THE VICTIM

"The church?"

"That's what I said, man. There's a whole lot of men working in there . . . One of them's just looked into the church tower and found a man."

"Our man?" asked Sloan, trying to keep a grasp of essentials.

"I don't know. You'd better get over there and find out."

"Dead or alive, sir?" It was as well to know . . .

"Dead." The telephone line crackled and went faint.

"What was that, sir?" asked Sloan. "I'm afraid I didn't quite catch . . ."

He recoiled as a great bellow came down the line. The interference on the telephone cleared as suddenly as it had started.

"Crushed to pieces," boomed Superintendent Leeyes. "Definitely dead."

Bantam Books by Catherine Aird
Ask your bookseller for the books you have missed

HENRIETTA WHO?
HIS BURIAL TOO
A LATE PHOENIX
A MOST CONTAGIOUS GAME
PASSING STRANGE
THE RELIGIOUS BODY
SLIGHT MOURNING
SOME DIE ELOQUENT
STATELY HOME MURDER

His Burial Too
Catherine Aird

BANTAM BOOKS
TORONTO · NEW YORK · LONDON · SYDNEY

All of the characters in this book are fictitious,
and any resemblance to actual persons,
living or dead, is purely coincidental.

*This low-priced Bantam Book
has been completely reset in a type face
designed for easy reading, and was printed
from new plates. It contains the complete
text of the original hard-cover edition.*
NOT ONE WORD HAS BEEN OMITTED.

HIS BURIAL TOO
*A Bantam Book | published by arrangement with
Doubleday & Company, Inc.*

PRINTING HISTORY
*Doubleday edition published October 1973
Bantam edition | January 1981*

ISBN 0–553–13949–5

Published simultaneously in the United States and Canada

---

*Bantam Books are published by Bantam Books, Inc. Its trade-
mark, consisting of the words "Bantam Books" and the por-
trayal of a bantam, is Registered in U.S. Patent and Trademark
Office and in other countries. Marca Registrada. Bantam
Books, Inc., 666 Fifth Avenue, New York, New York 10103.*

PRINTED IN THE UNITED STATES OF AMERICA

0 9 8 7 6 5 4 3 2

For
Jennifer, Peter, Jonty and Elizabeth
with love.

WHO HAS HIS BIRTH DAY,
    HAS HIS BURIALL TOO;
AS WE INTO THE WORLD COME,
    OUT WE GOE.
        Epitaph in Crundale Church

The chapter headings are taken from the plays of John Webster and Cyril Tourneur.

HIS BURIAL TOO

MEN OFT ARE VALUED HIGH, WHEN
THEY'RE MOST WRETCHED.

◆

1

It was the knocking which woke Fenella Tindall.

Not the first time it happened.

The first time the knocking came she was dreaming so deeply that she didn't even hear it. In her dream she wasn't tucked up safely at home in her own bedroom in the English village of Cleete at all. She was miles and miles away. In her dream she was in Italy. In Rome, to be exact. Walking down the Via Veneto with the two young Trallanti children.

It was in her dream as it had always been in real life—the pudgy little Nicola hurrying along beside her, her chubby hand tightly clutched in Fenella's, and the older and more adventuresome Giovanni skipping ahead of them both.

Nevertheless the knocking must have begun to register on her mind because her dream changed gear slightly.

She was calling to Giovanni now, telling him not to go too far ahead on his own. She had spent a lot of her time in Italy with the Trallanti children doing just that. She doubted whether in the long run anyone—anyone at all—was going to be able to keep Giovanni back. Already the boy was slim-hipped and handsome, and as lithe as quicksilver. And someday, too, not so many light-years away, his sister Nicola, dark, slow, and almost insultingly

1

good-looking, was going to break a heart or two.

Not that that was Fenella's problem.

Her problem had been teaching them English.

Fenella's own Italian was good—that had been how she had got the job in the first place—but she always spoke to the children in English. That was what their mother, the Principessa, wanted. That was how the English Miss Fenella Tindall of Cleete had come to be in Italy at all. To teach English to the Trallanti children.

"So that it is their second tongue, Miss Tindall," their mother had said firmly. "That is what I want."

And even that wasn't Fenella Tindall's problem any more.

Not now.

Not since she had had to come back to England again . . .

The knocking came again and this time it did reach her bedroom. The Italian dream faded. Her sleep-soaked mind forgot the Principessa and—in the infinitely accommodating way of dreams—tossed up an association to match the extraneous noise.

She was hammering away at something now—she wasn't quite sure what.

But urgently . . .

Now another figure appeared at the edge of her dream. A man, this time. She couldn't see him very clearly but again in the way of dreams she somehow knew who he was. Giuseppe Mardoni . . . She was aware of him there . . . small, dark, and engaging—and on the fringe.

There was another bout of knocking and she came one stage nearer true wakefulness. Another thought flitted through her mind.

"Wake Duncan with thy knocking . . ."

Then the sound—the real sound—came again and all the layers of unconsciousness were stripped away. She opened her eyes, admitted the world and was properly awake at last. The Trallanti children, Macbeth, and the insubstantial Giuseppe were all thoroughly banished by the present.

The present apparently consisted of someone knocking at the front door.

Fenella struggled out of bed and snatched at her dressing gown. It was a beautiful dressing gown—one which she had brought back with her from Rome and really cherished . . . she stopped suddenly. As she had been feeling about for her bedroom slippers her eye had fallen on her little bedside clock.

It said half-past eight.

She blinked.

It couldn't be as late as half-past eight.

Not half-past eight in the morning.

What about breakfast? What about getting her father off to work in Berebury? She shook herself. This wouldn't do at all. After all, the whole idea had been that something like this shouldn't happen. This was what she had come home from Italy for. To look after her father. She didn't seem to be making a very good job of it this morning.

She opened her bedroom door and shot along the upstairs landing. She called out to her father as she hurried downstairs to answer the door. Even in her present rush she was vaguely surprised that he wasn't already moving about. It really wasn't like him to sleep in quite as late as this—whether or not she was there to give him a call.

The knocking was coming from the front door all right. A renewed bout of it settled any doubts about that.

Fenella unlocked the door.

"Couldn't make anyone hear at the back," announced a short dumpy woman equably, "so I came round to the front."

"Oh, it's you, Mrs Turvey." Fenella pushed her hair back out of her eyes. "Come in. Thank goodness you woke me. We must have slept in."

"Happens to us all, miss, some time or other." Mrs Turvey lived farther down Cleete High Street and "did" for the Tindalls. She came in for a few hours every morning.

"I'd no idea it was so late . . ."

"Shouldn't be surprised myself if it wasn't the heat," said Mrs Turvey, stepping into the hall. "Ever such a hot night, it was. Not that it'll have seemed all that hot to you, miss, I expect. Not after that Rome."

Fenella smiled faintly. "No, it was just about right for me. What I remember of it." She had only been awake a matter of minutes but already she would have been hard put to it to say what it was that she had been dreaming about.

"Hot enough to make anyone oversleep in England, anyway," reaffirmed Mrs Turvey.

"You could be right about that—my father doesn't seem to have woken yet even," said Fenella, going back towards the stairs. "I'd better give him another shout now in case he didn't hear me come down."

"And I'd better put the kettle on." Mrs Turvey started off in the direction of the kitchen. "He can't go off, not without something inside him. Not even if he is late."

Fenella paused with one foot on the bottom step of the staircase as a new thought assailed her. "Mrs Turvey, you don't think that he's just gone out on his own without waking me, do you? You know, made his own breakfast and gone . . ."

"Well, it would be for the very first time, if he had, wouldn't it?" answered Mrs Turvey, not without spirit. "Had to be here b'half-past seven sharp, I did, until you came back home, miss. Every morning."

"That's true." Fenella nodded. No one could have called her father domesticated. Clever, good at his job, an admirable and devoted parent—all of those things. But domesticated—no.

That was the whole trouble. That was why she had come back home from Italy. She had been perfectly happy with the Trallantis in Rome but her father had been lonely and sad in England. She hadn't been able to bear the thought of him leading a solitary existence in Cleete . . .

"There's another thing, miss," said Mrs Turvey, rapidly unrolling the apron she had brought with her, "if he should happen to have got himself off on his own for once in a while . . ."

"Yes?"

"Then he's gone and locked all the doors behind him —which he wouldn't be likely to do seeing as how he knew I would be coming round soon the same as always."

"How silly of me," conceded Fenella quickly. "I hadn't thought of that." She turned and ran upstairs and then hurried along the landing to her father's bedroom. She tapped on the door.

There was no reply.

She knocked again.

"I'm afraid it's awfully late," she called out. "We've both slept in this morning."

There was still no answer.

She put her hand on the knob and opened the door. The bedroom curtains were still drawn against the light but the morning sun beyond them was coming in strongly enough for her to see quite easily that the bed was empty.

Not only empty but still made.

There was no sign whatsoever of her father in the room. More importantly, there was no sign whatsoever of his having been in there at all overnight. Everything was just as it had been when Fenella had gone in during the evening before to draw the curtains and to turn down the bed.

She took a second swift glance round the room and then went back on the landing and called down to Mrs Turvey.

"He's gone." She swallowed. "At least, he's not here."

Police Superintendent Leeyes landed the problem of the absent Mr Tindall of Cleete squarely on the desk of Detective Inspector C. D. Sloan (Christopher Dennis to his wife and parents, "Seedy" to his friends) not very long after that hard-working officer reported for duty at Berebury Police Station that morning.

The Thursday morning.

The Thursday after the Wednesday.

Everyone was to remember Wednesday, July 16th. That, at least, was one thing which helped the police. Wednesday, July 16th, was one of the hottest days in living memory in the county of Calleshire and it wasn't forgotten for a long time.

It had been really hot. Not just the ordinary warm weather which customarily passes for summer in England, but hot.

Workers in chocolate factories had had to be sent home

because the chocolate was unworkable. Sales of ice cream had soared along with the thermometer. By the middle of the afternoon it had been so hot that—over in the southeastern corner of the county of Calleshire—a fat man had attended a funeral without his jacket.

This particular disregard for the proprieties so incensed a retired major general (who didn't know what things were comin' to) that he wrote an indignant letter about it to the Editor of one of the local papers—*The Calleford Chronicle*. The police later read this in their patient attempt to build up a complete picture of the day in question.

The letter, predictably, triggered off an energetic correspondence which only finished—weeks afterwards—with a spirited letter from another mourner at the same funeral, who wrote that he was sure that the deceased would have been sympathetic towards the shirt sleeves (he was about to be cremated anyway)—and with a terse note from the Editor of the paper saying "This correspondence is now closed."

By the time that happened everyone in Calleshire knew the name of Richard Mallory Tindall.

The Criminal Investigation Department of Berebury Division, of which Detective Inspector C. D. Sloan was in charge, was small—all matters of great criminal moment being referred to the Calleshire County Constabulary Headquarters in the county town of Calleford. It did, however, collect—much to Sloan's regret—all the odd jobs.

This, it seemed, was one of the odd jobs.

"Man missing," announced Superintendent Leeyes briefly, waving a thin message sheet in his hand. "Seems as if he didn't go home last night."

"Can't say I blame him for that, sir," rejoined Inspector Sloan, fingering his collar. "Thank goodness it's better today."

The Thursday, as everyone—but everyone—remarked, mercifully was cooler than the Wednesday and almost everyone was relieved. Even those who had begun by lapping up the heat of the day before with a certain atavistic voluptuousness had ceased to wallow in it and begun instead to weary of it by evening. Hot nights were for sub-Mediterranean type peoples, not the English.

Superintendent Leeyes, who never admitted to changes of temperature on principle, grunted.

"Much too hot for sleeping in a bed," continued Sloan firmly. "I shouldn't have minded staying out myself last night, sir, come to that."

Leeyes glared at him. "Supposing he was that daft, too, and went down to Kinnisport for a swim in the moonlight or some such fancy carry-on in the dark then neither his clothes nor his body have turned up . . ." He paused and then added lugubriously, ". . . yet."

"He just didn't go home, sir?" enquired Inspector Sloan. "Er . . . is that all?"

The missing man—if he was missing—was by no means the only problem to fetch up on his desk. Like beach-combings washed up by the tide, other worries were stranded there too. There was a nasty little outbreak of anonymous letters over at the village of Constance Parva to be sorted out—to say nothing of the mysterious behaviour of the Berebury mayoral car. The funniest of things kept on happening to that—and always when the Mayor was sitting in it.

"That's all," responded Leeyes flatly. "He just didn't go home."

"But it's not a crime, sir," ventured Detective Inspector Sloan. For all that he was the titular head of Berebury's tiny Criminal Investigation Department Missing Persons didn't usually come within his province. "Not to go home, I mean."

"I know it's not," snapped Leeyes, "but he's officially been reported missing and we can't just write it down and forget it, can we, Sloan?"

"No, sir, but . . ."

"And what with your friend, Inspector Harpe, grabbing everyone on the strength who's capable of waving his arms about—and some who aren't—for his blasted traffic problems . . ."

"Yes, sir, but . . ."

"Not that a collection of scarecrows wouldn't do the job just as well for all the good they seem to do . . ."

"Quite, sir," agreed Sloan with feeling. Berebury's traffic jams were a byword in the county—and classic textbook in origin. A medieval town plan surrounded by twentieth century urban sprawl, the experts said. The police had a pithier way of putting it.

"That means," said Leeyes, coming triumphantly up the straight, "that there's only you and Detective Sergeant Gelven left not trying to sort out motorists."

"Yes, sir," repeated Sloan, subconsciously noting that even at a time like this the Superintendent didn't think Sloan's own most junior assistant, Detective Constable Crosby, was worth a mention. Those were Sloan's sentiments, too. The defective constable was what they called him at the Station . . .

The Superintendent threw his pen down onto the desk. "That's what police work's been reduced to, Sloan. Caning the motorist. Motoring law and motoring order. That's all anyone cares about these days. I never thought I'd live to see the day when . . ."

Detective Inspector Sloan cleared his throat and tried valiantly to get back to the point. "This chap, sir. How did we hear he was missing?"

"What? Oh, Police Constable Hepple told us. You know him, Sloan, don't you? He keeps everything nice and quiet down to the south—Larking way and round there."

Sloan nodded but said nothing. Her Majesty's Inspector of Constabulary might not define the duties of a police constable as "keeping everything nice and quiet" but it put the situation in a nutshell as far as the Superintendent was concerned.

"Hepple's stationed at Larking," the Superintendent was going on, "as you know, but he covers this little village of Cleete as well. And half a dozen others." Leeyes grunted. "Seems as if he bicycled over there this morning to pin up a notice in the church porch about warble fly . . ."

Sloan kept his face expressionless. Somewhere he had once read that there were really only half a dozen original stories in the world. He knew that *Cinderella* was one of them; the woodcutter's son and the Princess was another and—going back aeons before Aesop—the eternally fascinating tale of the Town Mouse and the Country Mouse.

He sighed.

Bicycling to the church to put up a notice in the porch about the dangers of warble fly to sheep was about as far removed from town police life as it was from the planet Mars. And being late with it into the bargain, thought Sloan suddenly. He might work in the town but he'd been brought up in the country. You dipped sheep earlier than this.

"The church porch?" he echoed dully.

"That's right. And that's where this chap's daily woman nabbed him with this story about her employer being missing." The Superintendent peered at the message sheet again. "The woman's name is Mrs Turvey. Apparently she went to the house this morning at eight-thirty like she always does and . . ."

"No chap?"

"Exactly," Leeyes grunted again. "Bed not slept in . . ."

"So it doesn't happen often then," deduced Sloan intelligently.

"Never before, apparently. Not without him saying. That's what's making her so worried. If he's ever delayed anywhere he always lets them know."

"Them?"

"There's a daughter." The Superintendent flipped over another sheet of paper. "Funny name she's got . . . here it is. Fenella."

"Fenella." Detective Inspector Sloan wrote that down in his notebook.

On a new page.

Every case had to begin somewhere.

Usually with a name.

"Anyway," persisted Leeyes, "Hepple says this Mrs Turvey told him that when Miss Fenella saw that the master's bed hadn't been slept in . . ."

Sloan kept his face straight with an effort.

It *was* different, all right, out there in the country.

". . . she called her upstairs and they both had a look for him. The daughter didn't know he wasn't in the house. She was expecting him to have come home after she'd gone to bed."

"I see, sir." He didn't see anything yet but he would. In time.

"That means you'll have to find him, Sloan, whether you like it or not."

"Yes, sir." Sloan cleared his throat and said, "But what about whether he likes it?"

"What's that? What did you say?"

"Can we be sure that he wants to be found?" That might make a difference. Sloan himself wouldn't have wanted to have been restored to the bosoms of some of the families he had known people have.

"Why not?" demanded the Superintendent, who was not given to finer family feelings.

"Like I said, sir, it's not a crime not to go home for the night."

Superintendent Leeyes looked quite blank.

"I mean, sir," amplified the Inspector patiently, "perhaps he's left his wife on purpose and doesn't want her to know where he is . . . "

"No," declared Leeyes triumphantly, "it isn't like that at all because he hasn't got a wife."

"I see, sir."

"Constable Hepple said so. And he knows everything about them all out that way."

Sloan nodded his understanding. This was what made Hepple a good man all right. They said that knowledge was strength. That would be how the singlehanded Hepple was able to keep everything nice and quiet in his own little territory to the south of Berebury.

"She died a few months ago," went on Leeyes. "Hepple says he's only got a daughter. Fenella. Miss Fenella Tindall."

"Tindall?" exclaimed Sloan suddenly, hearing the surname for the first time. "That rings a bell. Sir, would that by any chance be anything to do with that rather odd firm, Struthers and Tindall?"

It was the Superintendent's turn to nod.

"You know," went on Sloan hurriedly, "the people who have that works down near the Wellgate here in Berebury who call themselves something funny . . . "

"Precision, Investigation, and Development Engineers," supplied Leeyes.

"And who are always asking Inspector Tetley for extra security without wanting to tell us why."

"Everything to do with them," said Leeyes neatly. "That Tindall."

"Oh, dear."

"Exactly."

UNEQUAL NATURE, TO PLACE WOMEN'S HEARTS
SO FAR UPON THE LEFT SIDE!

◆

2

Busier by far than the Dower House at Cleete and a good
deal noisier than the Police Station at Berebury were
the works of Messrs Struthers and Tindall near the
Wellgate in Berebury. It was a long low building, all
on one floor and as orderly as a beehive. The perpetual
hum which could be heard even from the outside carried
the similarity still further. The resemblance, though,
ended at the laboratory door. Bees lived by instinct. They
didn't do experiments.

Miss Hilda Holroyd, private secretary to Mr Richard
Tindall, replaced the telephone receiver on her desk in
the office with a visible frown.

She thought for a moment and then went and tapped
on the door of the combined office and laboratory of
Mr Tindall's second-in-command. That was Mr Henry
Pysden, who was the deputy general manager and also
head of the scientific side of the firm.

Reluctantly.

Mr Pysden made no secret of the fact that he hated
being disturbed when he was working on an experiment
himself and she had been in to him twice this morning
already. The first time had been to enquire if he had
had any message from Mr Tindall to say he wasn't coming in which hadn't reached her.

13

He said he hadn't.

The second time had been to ask him if he would see an importunate visitor, Mr Gordon Cranswick, who had arrived on the doorstep and who was showing signs of not wanting to be fobbed off by her.

He said he wouldn't.

And had added: "If it's about the last batch of tests we did for him, tell him to see Paul Blake or one of the metallurgists. If it's anything else he'll have to wait and see Mr Tindall when he does get here. Or make another appointment."

"I've just rung Mrs Turvey at Cleete," she began this time.

"Turvey?" Henry Pysden's voice sounded quite blank. He lifted his head—it was dome-shaped and almost bald —and peered at her through his thick-lensed glasses. "Turvey? I don't know anyone called Turvey."

"Mrs Turvey is Mr Tindall's daily woman at the Dower House," explained Miss Holroyd patiently. "She says he's not there either and she's told the police that Mr Tindall's missing."

"Good idea," said the deputy general manager warmly.

Miss Holroyd looked distressed. "But something quite ordinary might have happened to him."

"And it might not." Henry Pysden tapped his pen on the desk. "I can't go looking for him, Miss Holroyd."

"No, Mr Pysden, of course not."

"Besides"—the man essayed a faint smile—"it's much more in their line than in mine."

She smiled back. "Yes, Mr Pysden."

That was very true. There was never any point in getting the shortsighted Mr Pysden to help to look for anything.

"If there is an expert," pronounced Mr Pysden, "I say get him. I always tell people that, Miss Holroyd."

"Yes, Mr Pysden." Miss Holroyd nodded. That was true. She had often heard him say exactly that to clients.

Just as often, in fact, as she had heard Mr Tindall say the exact opposite to the same clients.

With him it was definitely the other way round. He positively favoured the amateur approach. "Your amateur's not cluttered up with academic prejudice, Miss

Holroyd," Richard Tindall was fond of saying. "He hasn't read every single thing that has ever been written on the subject. The amateur sees a problem in its simplest form and it doesn't occur to him that it's insoluble."

"He'll turn up, I expect, soon enough," Henry Pysden was saying easily. "I shouldn't worry too much if I were you, Miss Holroyd. It's quite early still, you know."

"But it's not like Mr Tindall," she persisted.

"He was late yesterday morning," pointed out Pysden.

"That was the road works."

"Well, then . . ."

Miss Holroyd shook her head. "No. They're all finished now. I checked."

"The devil you did!" exclaimed Pysden. "Do you ever overlook anything, Miss Holroyd?"

Her expression was austere. "Not if I can help it, Mr Pysden."

"No, of course not," he said hastily, seeming somehow to retreat behind his glasses. "I am sure you don't. By the way, Miss Holroyd, now that you are here I wonder if you would let me have the office patent register? I need it for the Galloway contract."

"Certainly, Mr Pysden. I think Mr Blake is working on it this morning. I'll get him to send it along to you."

"Blake?" said the deputy general manager sharply. "What's he doing with the patent register?"

Miss Holroyd frowned. "I rather think he's working on the Harbleton Engineering problem."

"Not United Mellemetics?"

"United Mellemetics?" Miss Holroyd looked up. "He can't be working on that. Don't you remember? You've still got the United Mellemetics file, Mr Pysden."

Henry Pysden shook his head. "No, I haven't, Miss Holroyd. I gave the file and the report back to Mr Tindall yesterday morning. When we had our coffee together. I'd finished with it by then."

"That's funny." Miss Holroyd looked puzzled. "I'm sure it's not in the safe . . . "

Mr Pysden stared at her.

*   *   *

There was a tiny tinkle as Mrs Turvey replaced the telephone receiver in the hall at the Dower House at Cleete. Then she hurried back to the kitchen.

As she bustled along she called out urgently, "The milk, Miss Fenella. Do catch it before it boils over."

"I did," said Fenella Tindall.

She was sitting now at the kitchen table, both hands clasped round a cup of coffee, still in her dressing gown. It was an Italian dressing gown, rich in all the colours of the Renaissance. Her mind, though, was not on clothes. She looked up anxiously as the daily woman came back into the kitchen.

"That wasn't my father on the telephone, was it, Mrs Turvey?"

"No, miss, I'm afraid it wasn't."

"Oh . . ."

"It was Miss Holroyd from your father's works. She was wondering why he wasn't in this morning yet."

"Oh, dear."

"He didn't go off early after all, then," said Mrs Turvey, "that's one thing for sure."

"No."

"Not that I thought that he had done, I must say. He's not an early bird, your father. Never 'as been, not since I've known him."

"No," absently. Fenella frowned. "And that means he didn't stay the night there either."

Mrs Turvey's square kindly face registered concern. "Doesn't look like it, miss, though I'm sure there's no call to get that worried . . ."

"What did you say to her?"

"That he wasn't here and that it didn't look to us as if he'd been home at all last night. Do drink up some of that coffee, miss. There's never any good worrying on an empty stomach, that I do know."

Fenella obediently took a sip of coffee. And then another. She was surprised to find how thirsty she was.

And puzzled.

She had been back home long enough to know her father didn't make a habit of staying out all night without saying anything to anyone. Besides, he was very much a man who liked routine; everything at its proper time and in its proper place. This behaviour just wasn't like him.

"Poor Miss Holroyd," continued Mrs Turvey. "She said he's got someone there now who says she's got an appointment to see your father and she was beginning to get worried, too."

"She'll cope," said Fenella decidedly. "My father always says Miss Holroyd can cope with anything."

"That's as may be," said Mrs Turvey engimatically.

Fenella, undeceived by this, grinned. She knew all about the perpetual state of rivalry that existed between Mrs Turvey and Miss Holroyd, both as jealous as Malbecco. Fortunately each felt superior to the other—Mrs Turvey because she had been married; Miss Holroyd because she had been educated.

"Anyway," said Mrs Turvey, "it's a Mr Gordon Cranswick who's there. She said to ask if you knew anything about him, miss . . ."

Fenella shook her head.

"She was wondering if she'd made a mistake," said Mrs Turvey, "and Mr Tindall meant this Mr Cranswick to have come out here to Cleete to see him at home and that was why he hadn't gone in to the office this morning."

"Miss Holroyd doesn't make mistakes," chanted Fenella. It was a sort of litany she had learnt from her father.

"I'm sure I hope not," responded Mrs Turvey repressively. "Anyhow, she says Mr Pysden is all tied up with one of his timed experiments and so he couldn't see him instead of your father."

"Oh, dear."

"He's someone important, she said."

Fenella put down her coffee cup and said energetically, "I don't like the sound of that at all."

"There now, miss, don't say that. Your father'll turn up presently or give us a ring."

"Did you tell her," asked Fenella more diffidently, her head studiously bent over her coffee cup, "that we'd told the police?"

Mrs Turvey busied herself over the stove. "Well, I sort of hinted that I'd happened to mention it to Mr Hepple on account of me just happening to see him in the road beyond the drive when I answered the door to the post-man."

"Was she cross?"

"Not so much cross," said Mrs Turvey consideringly, "as a bit surprised." She straightened herself up. "Still, what's done is done and can't be undone."

"No. I mean, yes. You don't think he's just gone to London or anything like that, do you?" Fenella pushed the empty coffee cup away and answered her own question. "No, he'd have rung first thing to tell us, wouldn't he?"

She jerked her shoulder in a compound of anxiety and irritation. It was absurd to know so little about the habits of one's own parent but when you have been away from home so much and have not been back again very long . . .

"He'd have telephoned Miss Holroyd anyway," declared Mrs Turvey sensibly, "because of this Mr Crans-wick coming to see him 'specially. He wouldn't have forgotten him, not your father. Not unless he's gone and lost his memory or anything like that."

Fenella sighed. "I can't understand it at all. It's just not like him to go off like this without saying anything to anyone."

Mrs Turvey's mind was going off on quite a different tack. "I do wish he'd put on that clean shirt I left out for him yesterday morning, miss. I laid it out for him special."

"Yes, of course . . ." The laundry was one of the threads of life at the Dower House which Fenella hadn't yet gathered up into her own hands.

"I don't like to think of him in the one he had on, miss, whatever he's doing," she said, turning her attention to the kitchen sink. "And it wasn't for want of reminding, Miss Fenella. If I said to him once I said it a dozen times . . ."

"I know," Fenella assured her hastily.

Mrs Turvey sniffed. "Seemed to me that he didn't want to look smart on purpose yesterday. He put his old suit on, too."

"The grey." Fenella remembered that much.

"The grey with the button off the left sleeve," retorted Mrs Turvey, "which I left out to take to the cleaners come Friday. Not for him to put on yesterday morning. It wasn't even in his bedroom, miss. I'd put it out on that chest on the landing that your poor mother called something funny . . ."

"Ottoman . . ."

"Ottoman," repeated Mrs Turvey doubtfully, "so as it shouldn't be forgotten-like and before you could say Jack Robinson he goes and puts it on."

"I know."

"And when I said about it he said he was sorry and he'd put the other one on today." She splashed hot water into the washing-up bowl.

"I heard him." Fenella pushed back her chair and took her coffee cup over to the sink. "I don't think I can manage any toast this morning, Mrs Turvey. I'm not really very hungry."

The daily woman swept the coffee cup and saucer into the bowl of hot soapy water with a practised hand, and Fenella looked at her watch.

"Mr Osborne couldn't tell you anything, miss?"

"Not a lot," replied Fenella.

Her father had spent the evening before with George and Marcia Osborne in Berebury because she was going out with Giuseppe Mardoni on his last evening before he went back to Italy. He'd wanted her to go out. Urged her, in fact. He couldn't have her burying herself in the country forever. That's what he'd said. He would be quite happy, he had insisted, calling in on the Osbornes. He might even go round and keep old Walter Berry company for an hour or two afterwards.

Fenella had rung George Osborne at Berebury Grammar School where he taught physics as the boys were beginning to file into morning assembly.

"Just," said Fenella to Mrs Turvey, "that he told them he had someone to see on the way home."

"Not old Professor Berry, miss, do you think?"

That was just what Fenella had asked George Osborne.

"He didn't say who it was," the Physics Master had replied. "He left us about half-past ten and he was all right then. I shouldn't worry too much if I were you. He'll turn up. And Fenella . . ."

"Yes?"

"When he does will you give him a message for me?"

"Of course."

"Tell him that Marcia found her earring, will you?"

"George! She didn't lose Great-Aunt Hilda's earrings, surely, did she? Not the emerald and diamond ones?"

"The Osborne heirloom," he agreed solemnly. "At least, half the heirloom. One earring to be exact. Anyway, it wasn't lost after all. She's found it again, thank goodness. Last night. After he'd gone. Tell him, will you . . ." She had heard the school bell clanging in the background. "I must go now. Ring Marcia if you want."

Fenella hadn't rung Marcia. It was too early. The day didn't begin for the well-dressed Marcia Osborne until at least eleven o'clock.

Nor for old Professor Berry for that matter. Between his library and his chess set he never went to bed until the early hours of the morning and he rose equally late. His housekeeper bemoaned the fact up and down the village. It was no use ringing him either yet.

Fenella took another look at her watch and said instead: "That policeman should have had time to have rung the hospitals by now."

"Bless you, miss, you don't want to worry about him being in hospital. If your father had had an accident in that car of his—which I wouldn't suppose for one minute that he had had, a more careful driver not being on the road—we'd have heard by now for sure. There's not two cars like that one of his this side of Calleford."

Fenella managed a rueful smile, appreciating that Mrs Turvey was trying so very hard to be helpful. "That's true."

"And another thing—everyone knows that it's his." The daily woman swilled the water round the sink with vigour. "Cars like Mr Tindall's don't grow on trees."

Fenella started to toy with the tassel on the end of the cord on her dressing gown. "It's a funny thing, you know, Mrs Turvey, but I could have sworn I heard him come in last night as usual . . ."

Mrs Turvey shook her head.

". . . I was in bed," persisted Fenella. "I'd been home for about an hour and I was just in that dreamy stage. You know—half asleep and half awake—when you're certain you're going to fall asleep in a minute but you haven't quite got there . . ."

"I know, miss." Mrs Turvey had finished the washing up now and had begun to polish the taps over the sink.

"Well, I thought I heard his car last night, like I usually do. You know how he always changes down a gear for that sharp bend just before the garage—you can't get round without, not in that car . . ."

"It wasn't built for cars, that road."

"No," agreed Fenella, deciding that Mrs Turvey, at least, would have thoroughly approved of the horse-drawn *carrozzas* in Rome. "Well, with my bedroom being on that side of the house anyway . . ."

"No, miss." Mrs Turvey shook her head. "It wouldn't have been him. Not last night. First thing I looked for when you told me he wasn't in his room was the garage key. Your father always puts it on the hook by the garden door as soon as he comes in. Always. I've never known him not . . ."

Fenella forbore to say that she had never known her father not come home for the night either.

"I was just drifting off," she said instead. "I remember thinking 'Oh, good, he's home' and then I turned over and went to sleep."

"The key isn't there, miss. Must have been · the night before."

She nodded uncertainly. "I suppose so. Unless . . ." Fenella suddenly stood stock still in the middle of the kitchen floor. ". . . unless he got as far as the garage and then something happened."

"Oh, Miss Fenella, surely not."

Fenella girded up the long trailing skirts of her dressing gown. "I'm going to see."

"Wait for me, miss." Mrs Turvey snatched at a towel with wet, dripping hands. "Wait for me."

"Come on then. Hurry!"

"Now, don't you go down to that garage on your own . . ."

Fenella took no notice.

She opened the back door of the Dower House and sped across the lawn, her bedroom slippers brushing a faint trail over the dewy grass. She was closely followed by a slightly panting Mrs Turvey.

Both of them came to an abrupt halt in front of the garage doors.

"Why, miss, they're shut," declared Mrs Turvey in manifest surprise.

"That's funny," agreed Fenella. "They were open. I opened them myself yesterday evening while I was waiting to be called for."

Mrs Turvey nodded approvingly. "There's nothing your father hates more than having to get out of the car of a night to open them himself. A real nuisance, he calls that."

Fenella advanced.

"Now, don't you open them doors," entreated Mrs Turvey urgently. "Miss Fenella, leave them alone. Let me go in there first."

She was too late.

Fenella had already pushed the garage door open.

A long blue car stood there.

It was quite empty.

◆

3

Two matters conspired to delay Detective Inspector Sloan leaving Berebury Police Station for Cleete that morning.

The first was a sad disappointment for him.

He wasn't going to be able to take Detective Sergeant Gelven—the staid, resourceful, and utterly reliable Sergeant Gelven—with him after all. When Sloan sent for him it transpired that Sergeant Gelven had been summoned—literally—to attend the Assizes at Calleford, the county town of Calleshire.

"To give evidence, sir," reported Gelven regretfully, "in one of the nastiest cases of perjury I've ever come across."

Sloan groaned aloud.

"I'm very sorry, sir," said the sergeant. "I'm sure I don't know why they bother myself. The accused wouldn't know an ethic if he saw one, for a start. Not if he met it on the stairs, he wouldn't. He says," added Gelven drily, "that he doesn't understand the meaning of the charge."

"I'm not surprised," said Sloan, who knew the gentleman in question. "I don't suppose he does. Do you realise, Gelven, that that actually could be the truth?"

"First time he's spoken it in a month of Sundays, I'll be bound," said Gelven fervently. "And then by accident. Perjury wouldn't mean a thing to him."

"A real no-good boy-o . . ."

23

"That's the ticket, sir. If you happened to need some-one to sup with the devil for you, he'd be just the man for the job. Otherwise there's not a lot he's any good for, I'm afraid . . ."

"It means that I shall have to take Crosby with me instead," said Sloan anathematising the unnamed perjurer under his breath. He did not relish making do with Detective Constable Crosby instead of the sergeant. Crosby was young, brash, and the perennial despair of all those at Berebury Police Station who had dealings with him.

"And why aren't you being a traffic light for Inspector Harpe?" demanded Sloan with unwonted savagery when Crosby reported to him. "Everyone else is."

"I don't know, sir."

Sloan, who could guess, had told him to get the car out. "We are about to venture into the interior, Crosby . . ."

"You mean 'the hush,' sir," he said reprovingly.

Constable Crosby prided himself on being up to date with the new colloquialisms. This was one of the factors which made him unpopular at the Police Station.

"The hush," he repeated. "That's what it's called now, sir."

"Is it indeed?" Sloan had managed between clenched teeth—before going to check that nothing was known about Richard Tindall.

Nothing was.

Not "known" in the police sense, that is.

There was one rather odd incident on record, though, from the day before.

Odd in the circumstances, that is.

In the ordinary way there was nothing unusual about a man dropping by the Police Station to report traffic chaos. People were always doing just that.

Especially these days.

What was odd was that the man who had done it the day before had been called Richard Mallory Tindall.

It was Inspector Harpe who told Sloan about it.

"It was all because it was such a hot day yesterday," he began cheerlessly. Inspector Harpe had the misfortune to be in charge of the Traffic Division of the Berebury

Division of the Calleshire County Constabulary. He was known throughout the Force as "Happy Harry" on account of his never having been seen to smile. Inspector Harpe maintained that so far there had never been anything in Traffic Division at which to smile. "It doesn't suit me, the heat, Sloan, but it suits tar."

"Tar?"

"The Divisional Surveyor decided to resurface the road south. You know—the one between here and Randall's Bridge."

"I know." Sloan inclined his head. Cleete was one of a cluster of small villages beyond there. The roads from all of them crossed the river Calle at the village of Randall's Bridge.

"Well, yesterday might have suited his tar," grumbled Harpe, "but the blighter forgot it was Market Day here in Berebury."

"Oh, dear."

"Chaos," said the traffic man succinctly. "Absolute chaos. And every manjack of 'em who'd been grumbling about the state of the road ever since that bad frost we had back in February forgot every pothole there'd ever been while they waited to get past the steamrollers."

"More than one?"

"Two," said Harpe. "Doing a stately schottische, this chap Tindall said they were, fore and aft of the tar-spraying lorry."

"At nought miles an hour," said Sloan sympathetically.

"That wasn't all," groaned Harpe. "The roadmen went and got into a muddle with their flags. Roadmen!" He rolled his eyes expressively. "They might have been road-men but men of the road they most certainly were not. One of them had never ridden anything stronger than a bicycle in his life. The other one apparently gets a power complex every time anyone puts a red flag into his hand."

"How did you find all that out?"

Inspector Harpe looked gloomier than ever. "Had a bit of an up-and-a-downer with the Divisional Surveyor, if you must know. Asked him where he got his men from. He said he couldn't get 'em from anywhere and how were police recruiting figures."

"And then what?"

"Both these characters showed their green flags at the same time."

Sloan grinned at his colleague.

"It wasn't funny, I can tell you, Sloan. There was this chap Tindall's car sitting in between the two advancing steamrollers. Their drivers couldn't hear what was going on—you know what a din they make—and the foreman didn't want to know, what with all that hot tar about and everything."

"I don't blame him. Then what happened?"

"I gather Mr Tindall practically stood on his horn for a start. Then, he said, at the eleventh hour the inexorable gavotte changed into a majestic minuet."

Sloan looked up.

"That's just what he said," insisted Harpe, whose accurate verbal memory had stood him in good stead as a young police constable. As an Inspector in charge of traffic it served only to keep him awake of nights. "Full of dancing words, he was. He said that after that the two steamrollers crunched away from each other again—for all the world like retreating partners on a dance floor."

"Everything but the bow and curtsey," agreed Sloan.

"Then he dropped in here to let us know what it was like out there," finished Harpe. "A queue two miles long on the Berebury side. What it was like the other way, I daren't think, being Market Day and all."

"How did he complain?" enquired Sloan with interest. In his experience that told you more about a man more quickly than anything else.

"More in sorrow than in anger," said Harpe promptly. "Thought one of our chaps might soothe things down a bit. He hadn't said anything to the roadmen, if that's what you mean."

Sloan decided then and there that the unknown Mr Tindall possessed that rare quality, judgement, if nothing else. "What was he like?"

Harpe screwed up his eyes in concentrated recollection. "Seemed all right to me. Tallish, middle-aged—you know, going a bit grey at the edges—quite active, though. Got in and out of his posh car a jolly sight easier than I could have done." Harpe glanced down at his own portly figure: he enjoyed his tunny and his contour had not so much gone to seed as gone to pod. "Nice car, though, except for getting in and out of."

"One of those, eh?"

"Well, I must say I wouldn't have wanted a couple of steamrollers doing a nutcracker act on it if it had been mine. They don't give them away with a packet of tea. Anyway"—Harpe quickly reverted to his own troubles— "I couldn't send Jenkins because he was caught up with a flock of sheep on the Kinnisport road and Bailey was out teaching school kids how to be responsible traffic-minded citizens of the future—Heaven help us all—so I told Appleton to go out there and sort things out. A pity, but there wasn't anyone else available by that time. They were all around at the Market."

"A pity?"

"He was down keeping an eye on the Calleford road junction. That's always a bad spot on Market Days. I didn't think it would make a lot of difference in the long run if that did get snarled up yesterday."

In the event this was not so.

It did make a difference.

The obstruction of the Cleete to Berebury road and the snarling up of the Calleford junction on the outskirts of Berebury—the London road—were but two of the minutiae which were later to contribute to the building up of a complete picture of the day in question.

Sloan thanked Happy Harry and went on his way.

There was subsequently no doubt in the collective police mind that Richard Mallory Tindall of Cleete had been alive and well and in no sort of apparent difficulty at a quarter past nine on the morning of the day before— that is, Wednesday, July 16th.

Fenella Tindall had only just finished dressing when she heard a car turn in to the Dower House drive. She went straight down to the front door and answered it herself.

A well-dressed man stood there, shifting his weight

from one foot to the other, barely concealing his impatience as she opened the door to him.

"Mr Tindall?" he said as soon as he saw her. "Is this his house?"

"It is." The man was a complete stranger to Fenella. "But . . ."

"Will you tell him that I'm here, please?"

"Who . . . ?"

"Cranswick," he said crisply. Everything about him was crisp: from his regulation haircut down to the caps of his highly polished shoes. He produced an engraved visiting card with prestidigitatory swiftness: *Gordon Cranswick of Cranswick (Processing) Limited.*

Fenella took the proffered business card. "I'm very sorry, Mr—er—Cranswick. He's not here as it happens and . . ."

"That won't do, you know." Mr Cranswick shook his head from side to side. "Not for me. It's not good enough. Not now. I know exactly where I stand, you see, after yesterday. He must know that. He'll just have to see me now whether he likes it or not."

"He can't," she said.

"I must see him," said Cranswick peremptorily. "It's important, my dear. Very important."

"He isn't here," repeated Fenella.

"Where is he then?"

"I don't know."

"Come, come, now." Cranswick gave her a hard look. He was a squarely built, contained sort of man, with a mouth and chin which could only be described as firm. "There's nothing to be gained by playing about. What's the matter anyway? We agreed that it could all come out today. He doesn't usually keep me hanging about like this."

"He doesn't usually not come home for the night either," retorted Fenella vigorously.

Gordon Cranswick stopped as suddenly as if he'd been hit.

"Not come home? That's different. Why didn't he come home? Where was he last? Who was he with?"

"Friends. Some people called Osborne. As it happens. Not that that's got anything to do with . . ."

"After that," he interjected quickly, dismissing friends with a wave of his hand. "Where did he go after that?"

"I don't know," said Fenella steadily. "Not yet."

"What I don't like about this, Miss Tindall—it is Miss Tindall, isn't it?—is that your father promised . . ."

"He wouldn't break a promise," she put in swiftly. "You can count on that."

"I had to go back to town yesterday to see our bankers and tie things up with them but he promised to see me today as soon as I cared to get here."

"Then," said Fenella with dignity, "I am sure that he will as soon as he can."

Gordon Cranswick changed his stance on the Dower House doorstep and began more pompously: "It is a matter of some considerable importance to me, Miss Tindall, that I see your father at the earliest possible moment." He paused impressively. "I may say that it is important to you, too . . ."

"Perhaps," said Fenella helplessly, "Miss Holroyd at his office . . ."

"His secretary? I've seen her already. She's not saying anything either."

"Mr Pysden, then," suggested Fenella. "He's my father's deputy . . ."

"I know. He was too busy to see me," declared Cranswick. "Not that I blame him for that. He isn't going to like the new set-up and I daresay he knows it. I never have seen eye-to-eye with Mr Henry Pysden."

"What new set-up, Mr Cranswick?"

"Cranswick Processing have made an offer for Struthers and Tindall."

"An offer?" Fenella was visibly startled. "For my father's firm?"

"That's what I said. What's more, I think I may tell you that it's already been accepted."

"When?" asked Fenella faintly.

"Yesterday afternoon. That's when your father agreed to sell me Struthers and Tindall . . ." He brought his right fist down on his left one for greater emphasis ". . . lock . . ." smack ". . . stock . . ." smack ". . . and barrel."

I AM I' TH' WAY TO STUDY A LONG SILENCE.

◆

4

Twenty minutes after leaving Berebury Police Station Detective Inspector Sloan had brief cause to be grateful for the road works of the Divisional Surveyor.

The sudden chatter of loose surface stones hitting the underside of the police car was the only thing which persuaded Detective Constable Crosby to reduce speed— and then only fractionally—on all the journey south into the country. Sloan glanced up and noted where yesterday's tar spraying had left its mark on the road.

Crosby soon picked up speed again.

Sloan averted his eyes from the road.

Driving fast cars fast was the one thing—the only thing—which Crosby did seem to be good at, but he might be wrong. Disastrously wrong.

"Cleete's a long way out, sir," remarked the Detective Constable presently, putting his foot down still farther on the accelerator.

"I've got some beads for the natives," responded Sloan tightly. "Mind that tractor . . ."

"Bags of room," said Crosby easily.

Sloan ran the passenger window down and tried looking out of the side of the car instead. That let a bit of air into the vehicle, too. It was going to be another hot day like yesterday. The hedgerows flashed past.

"There isn't that much hurry," he said more mildly,

allowing his mind to drift back to his roses. He thought they were flagging a little after yesterday's great heat. June had been a disappointment from the point of view of weather—and it had come after the latest and driest spring in a decade. So only now—in mid-July—were his precious roses in really full flower. He was nurturing a truly magnificent bloom of Princess Grace of Monaco for the Horticultural Society's Show on Saturday . . .

"Coming into Cleete now, sir. What are we looking for?"

"A man."

"What's he done?" Crosby's view of police life was an essentially simplified one.

"Gone missing." With an effort Sloan withdrew his mind from contemplating his roses and opened his notebook.

"Perhaps he's been abducted," suggested Crosby cheerfully. "Like the Duke of Calleshire's daughter who was taken away by that disc jockey fellow last year. You remember, sir . . ."

"I remember," said Sloan repressively.

No one who read the Sunday newspapers was likely to have forgotten the antics of Lady Anthea. Or the agency pictures of Calle Castle with the drawbridge up and the portcullis down.

"That was ransom," Crosby reminded him, "except that the Duke wouldn't pay it. Said they were welcome to her."

"That was dowry," said Sloan firmly, "except that the Duke wouldn't pay it. If this is ransom . . ."

"Yes?"

"There has been no mention so far of a letter of demand."

"That doesn't mean a thing, sir," said the Detective Constable blithely.

"No?"

"If the family have had a note asking them to leave ten thousand pounds under the blasted oak at the crossroads at dead of night they aren't necessarily going to tell us."

"Aren't they, indeed?" said Sloan grimly. "Well, let me tell you they aren't going to get very far if they don't."

"Perhaps it's suicide then."

"No note has been mentioned to me," said Sloan austerely, "yet."

As far as he was concerned suicides and notes went together as inevitably as Tweedledum and Tweedledee.

"There was the river at Randall's Bridge," Crosby reminded him. "That was only three miles back."

"And a railway line," commented Sloan, who hadn't been thinking about roses all of the journey.

"Almost spoilt by choice, sir, isn't he?"

"Suicides always are," said Sloan mordantly.

Crosby tried again. "This chap, sir, is he a bad 'un, then?"

"I don't know that either yet." Sloan stirred irritably: Crosby watched too many Westerns and it showed. "I did a person check with Records before I left the Station . . ."

What was it fashionable in the business world to call bad records these days?

There was a phrase for it.

Derogatory data.

That was it.

"No joy, sir?"

"Criminal Records Office have no knowledge of him under the name of Tindall, if that's what you mean by joy, Crosby."

The Constable deigned to brake for a road junction. "Which way now, sir?"

"We want the Dower House," said Sloan. "Hepple says it's quite conspicuous. It's in the middle of the village High Street and almost next door to the church."

It didn't take long to find.

Cleete was a small village—a jumble of cottages, a shop or two, a bit of green, a public house, a garage— all set round a church. They could see the thin spire of the church as they drove into the village. After that the Dower House was easy enough to locate.

Beyond both the Dower House and the church was a rather splendid avenue of oak trees but Inspector Sloan didn't turn to see where it led to. His attention had been caught by something parked at the front gate of the Dower House.

A police bicycle.

Detective Constable Crosby brought the police car to a stop beside it with a wholly unnecessary screech of brakes, and said, "Looks as if the Flying Squad's beaten us to it, sir, after all."

"Constable Hepple," deduced Detective Inspector Sloan. "He must have come back for something."

Police Constable Hepple had indeed come back to the Dower House for something. He advanced towards the police car in evident relief.

"It's Mr Tindall's car, sir. Miss Tindall's just found it in the garage. She rang me up about it. Said she thought we ought to know it was there."

"It's a point," agreed Sloan.

A man and his car weren't quite as indivisible as a man and his horse but at this rate they soon would be.

"Blessed if I know what to make of it myself, sir." Constable Hepple tilted his helmet back. "Doesn't make sense to me. Still," he added fairly, "I reckon I should have gone straight out and looked in that garage for myself, sir, first thing, but when Ada Turvey said the key wasn't in its usual place . . ."

"I take it," said Sloan, cutting in, "that you can't see the garage door from the house?"

He had never been one for relishing recriminations and found he less and less inclined to it as he got older. It never did any good. That was one thing which life had taught him—but not, alas, Superintendent Leeyes—by now. His only regret was that it was one of life's later lessons.

"No, sir," replied Hepple, mopping his brow. "Not from the house. The garage is part of the stables now, converted-like, and of course they were always well to one side of the house because of the smell of the horses."

Sloan nodded.

There was no doubt that they were out in the country now . . .

"I've seen the car, sir," continued Hepple. "The keys are still in the ignition and the garage key that Ada Turvey was on about—the one that's always hung on the hook by the garden door—that's still in the lock on the garage door."

"Nothing else?"

"A gent turned up asking for him. A business gent by the sound of him. Name of Gordon Cranswick. Properly put out he was, from all accounts. Wanted to talk to Mr Tindall sooner than now and didn't see why he couldn't. Went off somewhere in his car as quickly as he'd come, Miss Tindall said."

"But there's still no sign of her father?"

"Not a sausage, sir." Hepple shook his head. "Seems as if he just vanished into thin air after he came home and before he went to bed last night."

" 'Twixt the stirrup and the ground,' too," murmured Sloan for good measure.

"Beg pardon, sir?" said Hepple.

Sloan cleared his throat. "Between the garage and the house."

"That's right, sir," said Hepple, scratching his chin. "Leastways, that's what it looks like."

"Quite so," agreed Sloan. "We must remember that things may not be what they seem."

This was a principle he was always trying his best to instil into Detective Constable Crosby.

He hoped he was listening.

"I can't find him in the garden, though," went on Hepple doggedly, "and Miss Fenella and Ada Turvey they say they can't find him in the house." He jerked his shoulder towards the building behind him. "Mind you, sir, it's not all that small a house . . ."

No, it was not a small house. Sloan could see that himself. It was a very finely proportioned one, though. In fact, he had to take a second look at it before he realised quite how perfect it was.

"What they call Georgian, sir, I'm told," said Hepple, "on account of all the straight lines."

Sloan nodded. There wasn't a Victorian twiddle or bump in sight. And all—as the estate agents' optimistic advertisements said—well-maintained in excellent condition.

Hepple's arm described a circle. "And definitely a big garden."

Sloan grunted. There was no doubt about the size of the garden. You could have lost a platoon in it—easily—let alone one man.

"Best part of a couple of acres, sir, I'd say. At least."
Hepple ran an experienced eye over the grass. "And he
could be anywhere in that orchard at the back—anywhere
at all. Especially if he'd been taken ill after he got back
home last night."

Detective Inspector Sloan had no time for euphemisms
so early in the morning.

He looked at his watch and said briskly: "If he's been
on a real bender he could still be sleeping it off somewhere. It's not very late in the day yet."

"No, sir," said Police Constable Hepple, equally firm.
"He wasn't that sort of a drinker."

Sloan looked up quickly, realising that he'd come within an inch of underestimating a village constable; and
that would never do.

"If he had been like that, sir," Hepple went on seriously, "I wouldn't have reported him as missing at all
to Berebury. Not until much later on, sir, anyway, when
I could have been quite sure."

"I understand," said Sloan.

And he did.

With the warble fly and the church porch and the
bicycle there went a finer discrimination—and a greater
freedom—than you were able to have in the town.

It was at that moment that the front door of the
Dower House opened. Inspector Sloan turned his head
and saw a girl—a young woman, rather—standing there.
She was framed by the classical lines of the Georgian
doorway. She stood quite still as she regarded the three
policemen. There was something a little unexpected about
her appearance—almost foreign. It took Sloan a moment
or two to pin down what it was—and then it came to him.

It was her clothes.

It was high summer in England and this girl was wearing dark brown. Not a floral silk pattern, not a cheerful
cotton, nor even a pastel linen such as his own wife,
Margaret, was wearing today. But dark brown. It was a
simple, utterly plain dress, unadorned save for a solitary
string of white beads.

He was surprised to note that the whole effect was
strangely cool-looking on such a hot day. There was the
faintest touch of auburn in the colouring of her hair

which was replicated in the brown of the dress. A purist
might have said that her mouth was rather too big to be
perfect but . . .

Sloan wasn't a purist.

He was a policeman.

On duty.

He took a step forward.

"Have you found my father?" she asked him directly.

They were barely inside the Dower House when Mrs
Turvey came hurrying along the hall, wiping her hands
on her apron.

"There's a gentleman on the telephone," she said, "asking for a Detective Inspector Sloan. Said there was no
answer from the car radio or something. Sounds in a
terrible rush, 'e does . . ."

It wasn't a gentleman. It was Police Superintendent
Leeyes.

"That you, Sloan? Look here, we've just had a message from Randall's Bridge . . ."

"The river?"

"The river?"

"Or the railway line, sir?"

"What are you talking about, Sloan?"

"This message, sir."

"I'm trying to tell you it's from the church."

"The church?"

"That's what I said, man. There's a whole lot of men
working in there. They're putting in heating or something.
One of them's just looked into the church tower and
found a man."

"Our man?" asked Sloan, trying to keep a grasp of
essentials.

"I don't know. You'd better get over there and find
out."

"Dead or alive, sir?" It was as well to know . . .

"Dead." The telephone line crackled and went faint.
"Definitely dead."

"What was that, sir?" asked Sloan. "I'm afraid I didn't
quite catch . . ."

He recoiled as a great bellow came down the line. The interference on the telephone had cleared as suddenly as it had started.

"Crushed to pieces," boomed Superintendent Leeyes.

◆

5

Whatever time and distance record Detective Constable Crosby had set up on his way from Randall's Bridge to Cleete he broke on the return trip from the Dower House at Cleete to the church at Randall's Bridge.

Sloan hung on to the side of his seat for dear life as Crosby cornered. Police Constable Hepple they had left behind at Cleete with Fenella Tindall and Mrs Turvey.

Sloan spotted the church at Randall's Bridge easily enough. It was sited on a small prominence beside the river, its tall tower standing four square to the world for all to see.

Crosby swept the police car round the last corner and brought it to a shuddering stop behind a lorry loaded with pipes which was parked near the lych gate. Sloan tumbled out and set off through the churchyard. There was a small knot of men clustered round the church doorway. He noticed that they were dressed in working overalls and some still had tools in their hands. Two of the men were bending over a youth who was sitting on the grass of the churchyard looking more than a little green.

"Police," said Sloan.

One of the men jerked his thumb. "The gaffer's still inside. We brought Billy here out for a bit of air."

"It was Billy what found him," said another.

Sloan didn't need telling. He'd seen that shocked, in-

39

credulous look before. When someone had seen something not very nice, and didn't really want to take it in.

"Didn't believe him at first," said an older man.
"Thought he was having us on. You know what apprentices are."

Sloan nodded. He knew all right.

There wasn't a policeman alive who didn't know what
apprentices were.

He made his way past them to the church door, Crosby
at his heels. It was unlatched but nearly closed. He put
his shoulder to it and the great oak door swung open. He
stepped down into the church. At least it was cool enough
in here.

The first sight which met him was of apparent disorder
everywhere. It needed a second glance to see that this
was organised chaos—the work of the workmen. There
were pipes and boards everywhere. Some of the pews
were awry and there were dust sheets over the rest.

There were two more men standing by the door which
led to the foot of the church tower.

"Police," said Sloan again. "Detective Inspector Sloan."

"This way," said one of them thickly. "Over here."

"There's been a nasty accident," said the other.

Sloan advanced across the nave towards them, Crosby
clattering along behind him like some ghastly material
Doppelgänger.

"The door won't open above an inch or two, Inspector,
but you can just see inside." The shorter of the two men
stepped back from the doorway. "You look . . ."

Sloan looked.

Crosby, who was taller, looked too, over Sloan's
shoulder—and let out a long low whistle entirely contrary to his police training in professional impassivity.

The sight which had turned Billy, the apprentice, green
was a curious one.

The entire base of the church tower seemed to be full
of a vast quantity of smashed marble. There was one
great melange of broken white sculpture—here a foot—
there a head—all heaped on the floor. This was what was
preventing the door from opening more than an inch or
two.

There was also an arm which wasn't made of white marble.

It was clothed in men's suiting and was protruding from under all the heaped stone. The skin of the hand was pale and bloodless and though the light was poor Sloan was in no doubt at all that its owner was dead.

Like the Superintendent had said.

Definitely.

It was not all that easy to see anything else. There was a sort of ecclesiastical dimness about the inside of the tower.

"The light switch is inside, I suppose," he said.

"It is," said one of the men. "Not that it would be much of a help if we got to it, would it? Look."

Sloan's gaze travelled upwards. An empty light socket dangled under a Victorian fluted glass shade.

"No bulb."

"Poor devil," said the shorter of the two. He had a foot rule sticking out of his jacket pocket.

"At least," said the other man, "he never knew what hit him. Can't have done." This man was older and was neatly dressed in country-style tweeds.

Sloan cleared his throat. "Er—do either of you happen to know exactly what it was that did hit him?"

"The Fitton Bequest," responded both men in unison.

"Quite so," said Sloan.

It wouldn't do for the Superintendent; not an answer like that. He'd have to think of something better than that for his report.

"We put it in here last week, didn't we, Mr Knight?"

"That's right, Bert," the elderly man nodded. "You did. Bert Booth here is the foreman, Inspector."

"Took twelve men to move it," confirmed Bert, "and then we had a proper job."

"We went through all the necessary formalities first, Inspector," the man called Knight hastened to assure him, "before we touched it. Got a proper faculty for moving it, advertised, and so forth. I'm glad we did now. The Archdeacon would have been down on us like a ton of bricks if . . ."

Mr Knight suddenly realised that perhaps this wasn't

the happiest of similes and his voice trailed away to silence.

Inspector Sloan turned to Constable Crosby. "Get Dr Dabbe from Berebury out here as quickly as possible— and Dyson and the photographic people."

"Yes, sir."

"And on your way out tell that gang by the church door that if they move so much as an inch from where they are now then I'll run the lot of them in."

"Yes, sir." Crosby clattered away again.

Sloan turned back to the narrow slit which constituted their only view into the base of the tower. It was a bit limiting. All they would be able to do was what the archeologists called a pre-disturbance survey. They couldn't get near enough to disturb anything. He took another look at the arm. There wasn't a lot of it to see but it told him all he wanted to know.

It was a left arm.

It was contained in a length of men's suiting—grey suiting—and from where Sloan was standing it was possible to see that there was a button missing from the sleeve.

Fenella Tindall sat straight up in her chair as Police Constable Hepple came back from the telephone, her back every bit as stiff as the Principessa's.

In a way, the ringing of the telephone bell had come as something of a relief.

She had tried sitting in the garden while Constable Hepple had plunged about the orchard and found she couldn't do it. The house itself had been hardly more restful. True, there was no one in it but herself and Mrs Turvey but the impulse to go through all the rooms all over again was very strong.

So was the desire to shout aloud for her father—to call out and to listen for an answer.

She turned her head as Hepple came into the room. "Was that . . ."

Hepple said, "The Inspector, miss. It was a message from the Inspector."

"Any news?" She looked at him eagerly. "Is there any news?"

"Nothing definite, miss," temporised the policeman. "We'll let you know as soon as we have anything definite."

Fenella relaxed fractionally. "Then what . . ."

"It was about your father's clothes, miss."

"But I told you before."

"Just checking, miss, that's all."

"He was wearing a grey suit, like I said."

"A grey suit . . ."

"Not his best one," she pointed out quickly. "Mrs Turvey says there was a patch of grease on the right trouser leg. Is that any help?"

"Not exactly, miss." Hepple coughed.

It wasn't, either.

"Not at this stage," he added truthfully.

"That's why it was going to the cleaners, you see."

Hepple looked down at his notebook. "You said something else to me about it, miss, before . . ."

"There was a button missing."

"Where from?"

"The sleeve."

"Which sleeve?"

"The left one."

Hepple kept his eyes on his notebook. "You wouldn't by any chance happen to have that button, miss, would you? You know, ready for sewing back on again after the suit came from the cleaners . . ."

Something of the colour went out of Fenella's face but she kept her voice steady with an effort. "The button?"

"It would be a great help, miss, if we might have it . . ."

"I should like now," announced Detective Inspector Sloan to Mr Knight, "to take a look at the outside of the tower."

"But what about this poor bloke?" interjected Bert Booth, the foreman. "Aren't we going to try to get him out then?"

"How?" enquired Sloan.

"I've got plenty of men outside. You know that. They'd . . ."

"If they all heaved together," said Sloan, "we'd never get this door open. There must be all of half a ton of marble up against the back of it."

Bert Booth scratched his head. "That's a thought, guv'nor. But what about the other door? The churchyard one . . ."

The man called Knight shook his head at this. "You wouldn't be able to shift that one, Bert. No matter how hard you pushed. You can see what's up against the inside of it from here."

"Crikey," exclaimed Bert Booth, "then how on earth . . ."

"Quite so," said Sloan sedately.

Mr Knight stared at Sloan. "But that means, surely, Inspector, that no one can have left the tower after this happened—that he was alone in here when . . ." He fell silent.

"It does," agreed Sloan. "That's why I want to look round outside now."

The heat of the day struck him in full force again as he followed Mr Knight and Bert Booth out through the church door.

Billy, the apprentice, was looking slightly less green.

"Want to tell me about it now?" asked Sloan gently.

The boy gulped. "I was just looking, mister. That's all. And then I saw this arm sticking out. I didn't mean any harm, going in there."

"No."

"Honest, I didn't," he insisted earnestly. "When the door wouldn't open above an inch or two I looked to see what was keeping it. I didn't sort of take in the arm at first if you know what I mean."

"Then what did you do?" Sloan wasn't worried too much about the boy. His tale would lose nothing in the telling. By evening it would be as remembered with advantages as any Agincourt story—his genuine squeamishness talked out of him and forgotten. By tomorrow he would be a hero in his own small circle.

"I didn't touch anything."

"Except the door handle."

Billy looked crestfallen. "I'd forgotten about that."

"You weren't to know," said Sloan. "Then what?"

"I ran and told Mr Booth and he sent someone for Mr Knight."

It was Mr Knight who now led the way through the churchyard and round the outside of the church. It emerged that he was a retired schoolmaster and also secretary of the Parochial Church Council.

"That's why they sent for me," he explained. "I only live down the road. Here we are . . ."

Sloan stopped and took his first good look at the church tower. It was square and had just the one pair of double doors opening onto the churchyard. Set above the rounded arch of the doorway was a small window.

Bert Booth, the foreman, looked up at it and shook his head.

"That's not big enough to get anyone through to let us in from the other side. We couldn't even push Billy through that. He's not that little."

"No," conceded Sloan. The window was scarcely more than a slit to give light but not access: not even to the apprentice in his traditional role of being squeezed through narrow places.

"Typical Saxon," Mr Knight, the schoolmaster, informed him. "The whole tower is Saxon except the battlements at the top."

"Really, sir?" said Sloan courteously.

If there was one thing which Superintendent Leeyes would not want to know it was the age of the tower.

"We might get a better view with a ladder," said Bert Booth, the foreman, more practically. He disappeared round the other side of the tower.

"Saxon," said Mr Knight again. "Built about the time of the first bridge here." He indicated the river flowing beyond the church.

"Randall's Bridge?" said Sloan.

"Randalla the Saxon's Bridge, actually."

Sloan nodded. Pedantry will out.

"Before that there was a ford. The Romans used the ford."

"Did they, sir?" murmured Sloan absently.

So the Romans got their feet wet and the Saxons didn't.

That was progress, wasn't it?

Or just history?

"We don't know the exact place of the ford, Inspector. The river bed's shifted a bit since then." Knight inclined his head in the direction of the river Calle which ran along below them. One of the churchyard paths led down towards it. "Two thousand years is a long time."

"Yes, sir," said Sloan. So was twelve hours in a case like this. He peered up at the tower.

Knight pointed. "You can see the long and the short Saxon stonework at the corners, can't you, Inspector?"

"So you can, sir."

As it happened Sloan hadn't been considering the Saxon stonework, but long ago he had discovered that the one thing to do with antiquarians was to let them say their piece while he thought about something else. He was thinking now about the gravel outside the tower doorway. There was a certain amount of scuffing there—about six feet in front of the doors and below the window.

"It's a common Saxon feature," went on the schoolmaster happily, "to have the cornerstones alternately horizontal and vertical."

"Don't step on the gravel just here, sir, will you? I shall want some pictures taken of the gravel."

"You only get stonework like that in the Saxon period."

"Can you get out on the roof, sir?"

"From inside? Oh, yes, Inspector. Certainly you can. It's quite a climb up there round the bells but it can be done by anyone who is—er—reasonably agile. Haven't been up there for some time myself but there's a very good view from the top. On a clear day you can see Calleford."

Sloan stared up at the battlemented top of the tower.

From a view to a death in the morning?

Was that what it was going to be?

He didn't even know whether the death had been in the morning yet . . .

"When would the church have been locked?" he asked abruptly.

"Eleven o'clock, Inspector. I locked it myself just after eleven. I do it every night. When I take the dog for a walk."

"Dog?" sharply.

"Spaniel. Tessa."

Sloan expired. "Pity it wasn't a bloodhound."

"She's pretty good," protested the dog owner in injured tones.

"Did she know that he was in there?"

Knight frowned. "Now that you come to mention it, Inspector . . ."

Sloan sighed. That was never as good as the spontaneous remark. Unprompted, that was how statements should be.

". . . she did sniff round here. I didn't take a lot of notice at the time."

"Here? You came this way?"

"Yes. Up from the village street by the river path."

Sloan pointed to a cottage on the edge of the churchyard. "Is that your house, sir?"

"What? Oh, no. That's Vespers Cottage. The two Misses Metford live there. I'm over on the other side. That house opposite lych gate . . ."

"Then why did you come this way at all?"

For the first time the schoolmaster seemed to be at a loss for a phrase. He cleared his throat several times. "I—er—dropped in to The Coach and Horses actually to have a pint and a chat . . ."

"And you opened up this morning—when?"

"Just after eight. For the workmen."

There was a heavy scrunching sound round the far side of the tower and Bert Booth reappeared. He was carrying a ladder.

"That's funny," exclaimed Mr Knight suddenly. "Where did you find that ladder, Bert?"

"Lying along the wall. Reckon we can get up to that window with it, Inspector?"

"But," insisted the schoolmaster, "that ladder shouldn't have been left lying about outside like that."

"No, sir, it shouldn't." Sloan couldn't have agreed with him more. Ladders left lying around were always an anathema to the police.

"It's always kept in the tower," insisted Mr Knight. "Always."

Bert Booth shrugged his broad shoulders. "Well, it isn't there now and it wasn't one of my chaps who took it out.

We've no need of ladders, Mr Knight, you know that. Not on this job."

The ladder wasn't long enough to reach the top of the tower. There was no question of that. No one could have come down from the tower by it. But it was tall enough to have reached the aperture above the door.

Bert Booth turned to Sloan. "Do you want to have a shufti through that window up there, Inspector, or not?"

"Later," said Sloan. "When we've taken a cast of the gravel."

"Like that, is it?" said the foreman.

Sloan nodded.

◆

6

"I think sir," began Inspector Sloan cautiously, "that we may have found Mr Tindall."

As soon as Constable Crosby had returned to the church Sloan had gone to report back to Superintendent Leeyes at Berebury Police Station.

He'd got his police priorities right long ago.

He was using Mr Knight's telephone. Crosby's police car radio wasn't quite private enough for this sort of conversation. As he dialled Sloan could hear the schoolmaster pacing up and down in the other room, together with Bert Booth, the foreman.

Booth was waiting his turn to use the telephone to tell his employers—a firm of central heating engineers in Berebury—that there had been what he called "a bit of a hold-up." It didn't seem to have bothered the workmen. They were settling down to another tea break—this time in the churchyard. Sloan could see them and their mugs from the window of Mr Knight's sitting room.

Crosby he'd left behind inside the church.

Not that you could very well call him a "scene-of-crime officer."

Not Crosby.

A familiar grunt at the other end of the line indicated that the Superintendent was listening.

49

"We can't be sure, sir, of course, yet, but . . ."

"Too much of a good thing if not," responded Leeyes robustly. "A missing man and a dead one in one day in one Division. This isn't Chicago."

"No, sir . . ." he hesitated.

"Well, Sloan," barked the Superintendent, "are you going to tell me what happened or aren't you?"

"It's not all that easy to say, sir."

"I may not be 'Listening With Mother,' " said Leeyes heavily, "but I am 'Sitting Comfortably.' "

Sloan took a deep breath. "It's like this, sir. They're putting central heating in the church at Randall's Bridge . . ."

"What for?" The Superintendent was nothing if not a realist.

"Someone left them the money to do it. Just the heating. For that and nothing else. A specific legacy in a will . . ."

Sloan could hear the Superintendent muttering something cynical under his breath about fire insurance but he took no notice.

". . . a local boy who made good," he said, pressing on, "in Australia."

"Funny place to think about heating."

"He never forgot how cold it used to be in the church when he was a lad," said Sloan, repeating what the church secretary had told him. "He made a small fortune out of sheep, and he remembered Randall's Bridge in his will."

Leeyes grunted. "Go on."

"To get the pipes in properly the central heating people had to move a whacking great sculpture in the church—in the south aisle. A sort of monument, it was . . ."

"Was?"

"Was," affirmed Sloan remembering the arm underneath.

There was something terrible about that arm sticking out like that.

"Well?"

"It was a weeping widow and ten children all mourning the father. You know the sort of thing, sir."

"I do. Very upsetting they are, too," said Leeyes. "They don't allow them any more. And quite right."

"This one's called the Fitton Bequest. A memorial to remember Mr Fitton by . . ."

"I should have thought myself," remarked Leeyes, "that ten children were . . ."

"The workmen moved it into the church tower last week," went on Sloan hastily, "so that they could get on with laying the pipes and so forth. On its plinth. That's a good few feet high for a start. This sculpture stood on top of that."

"Hefty."

"I'll say, sir. It only just went through the door." Sloan paused. "I'm very much afraid that Mr Tindall is under what's left of it. And if it's not him, then it's somebody else . . ."

"Who's equally dead," grunted Leeyes, "which from our point of view . . ."

"Just so, sir." The police point of view wasn't everything but it was the one which they both had to worry about.

"This sculpture, Sloan . . ."

"Yes, sir?"

"What was keeping it on its plinth?"

"Gravity, sir. As far as I could see, that is."

"Gravity." He grunted again. "You can't play about with that, can you?"

"No, sir." That was true. Not even the Superintendent could play about with gravity.

"Well, then, did this Fitton thing . . ."

"Bequest."

"Bequest. Did it fall or was it pushed?"

Sloan took a deep breath. "I'm afraid it's not quite as simple as that, sir."

"It isn't," demanded Leeyes suspiciously, "going to turn out to be one of these fancy suicides, Sloan, is it? I can't stand them."

"I don't somehow think so, sir." It didn't look like suicide—however fancy—to Sloan. Not with the river and the railway line so hard by, so to speak.

"Firm not going to pot or anything like that?"

"Quite the reverse, sir, from all accounts. I'm told

there's a character who came to Cleete this morning who swears he was told that he could buy it outright yesterday. He's still as keen as mustard from what I hear."

"Is he now?"

Sloan heard that register at the Police Station all right, and added, "Cranswick's his name. Gordon Cranswick."

"Gordon Cranswick."

"We'll have to check, sir, of course."

"Of course."

"I don't think, sir," went on Sloan more slowly, "that whoever is under this marble could very well have pulled the thing down on top of himself at the same time as ending up face downwards underneath it. Not easily."

"Agreed."

"And we can tell he's lying prone because of the hand." Sloan was still amazed at what you could tell from a solitary hand.

"Well, then . . ."

"But if it was pushed, sir . . ."

"Yes?"

"There's a snag."

"I'll buy it, Sloan."

"If it was pushed . . ."

"Get on with it, man."

"Whoever did the pushing must still be in the church tower."

"Say that again, Sloan."

"No one's come out of that tower since the sculpture came down on that chap." Sloan spelled it out for him. "They can't have done."

"What!"

"There's half a ton of marble up against the far door— the one that leads to the churchyard."

"The west door," said Leeyes surprisingly.

Sloan blinked. "That's right, sir."

"Civic services," explained the Superintendent elliptically. "Have to go to a lot of them."

"Quite, sir. Well, there's nearly as much marble behind the pair of doors which give to the church itself from the tower. No one," he added carefully, "can have opened either set of doors from the inside after the sculpture came down."

"The roof?" Leeyes seized on the only alternative to the doors. "What about the roof?"

"There is a hatch leading out onto the roof," reported Sloan, "but the door up there is always kept locked—anyway, it's a long way up from the outside. Too far for ladders. And the church secretary has just shown me the key of the hatch—here in his house . . ."

He had also introduced his wife to Sloan. She was a drab, complaining woman, who immediately explained the need for voluntary jobs, a dog which required a lot of exercise, and any number of trips to The Coach and Horses.

Last night she had had one of her bad heads and had retired to bed early. She had seen nothing and nobody. When she had one of her bad heads she always went straight to bed . . .

Sloan wasn't worried.

When he had been over by the church tower he'd seen a curtain twitch in the window of the cottage there. Vespers Cottage, Knight had called it. Curtain-twitchers usually had something to report. He would go back there as soon as he could . . .

"I can't check the roof, yet, sir," he said into the telephone, "because I can't get in myself, but there's no doubt that it's too high for ordinary ladders and there's no rope hanging down there or anything like that."

The Superintendent groaned irritably. "Not another of those locked room mysteries, Sloan, I hope. I can't stand them either."

Fenella Tindall found it more difficult to sit still when Police Constable Hepple came back from the telephone a second time.

He had taken the button from her, measured it carefully, and then gone through to ring a number in Randall's Bridge.

That was all she knew.

That was all he had told her.

She took a deep breath now as he entered the room. "Well?"

"Have you got any friends, miss, here in the village?"

She felt a cold shiver run up and down her spine. She shook her head mutely.

"Someone who would come round," he continued kindly, "to be with you today."

"Not really. You see, I've only just come home from Italy. And I've been away so much."

"A friend of your father's, perhaps, then, miss? Who you would like to be with you . . ."

Obediently she cast about in her mind and then shook her head again. Marcia Osborne was a friend of her father's, all right, but Fenella couldn't see Marcia's charm. It was too brittle. George Osborne was a poppet, but he would be teaching now. There was always old Professor Berry, of course. He'd be up and about by now. But she could hardly expect him to be a prop and stay. Not at his age. And Miss Holroyd—staunch, rocklike and competent—Miss Holroyd would have enough on her hands as it was.

Police Constable Hepple was saying something.

"You were out with a friend last night, miss, I understand . . ."

Fenella looked up quickly. The constable might have seemed quiet and slow but . . .

"That was an Italian friend," she said, "called Giuseppe Mardoni. But he's gone back to Italy. He went last night. After we'd had dinner. He had to catch a plane. A night flight."

She was talking too much. She knew that.

To stave off the moment when the policeman said what he wanted to say.

What he had to say, sooner, or later.

"You see," she said, "I'm quite alone now."

"I see, miss. Well, then, in that case . . ."

"I think," said Fenella with a visible effort, "that I'd rather be told anything you know now . . ."

Hepple told her.

By the time Detective Inspector Sloan got back to the church the real experts in death had begun to arrive.

Constable Crosby might have fancied his fast driving but it wasn't a patch on that of Dr Dabbe. The Consultant Pathologist to the Berebury and District Group Hospital Management Committee was the fastest driver in the county of Calleshire. There was no doubt about that. Strong men had been known to blench when offered a lift by him. Those who incautiously accepted them were rumoured never to be the same afterwards. The Dean of Calleford, a blameless man whose faith was seemingly as firm as that of anyone in the diocese, had once tried to get out of Dr Dabbe's moving car, wishing he had led a better life the while. The doctor's assistant, Burns, who went with him everywhere, had been shocked into silence by it long ago and rarely spoke.

Sloan greeted him inside the church.

"I'm sorry, Doctor. We've got a body here for you all right but we can't get near it. And all we can see is an arm."

"No sword?"

"N . . . no, Doctor."

Dabbe gave a sardonic grin. "I was thinking of Excalibur."

"No, Doctor. No sword." Sloan managed a wan smile. The pathologist was always like this. He had a sense of humour fit to make your blood run cold. "The arm's lying quite flat, actually. Not—er—er brandishing anything."

"Ah . . ." Dr Dabbe advanced towards the tower doorway. "And all I've got is a sort of leper's squint, is it?"

"I'm afraid so." Apologetically. "They've sent to Berebury for some heavy welding equipment. They're going to try to cut the door hinges off from this side."

Dr Dabbe bent down and looked into the tower through the gap in the doorway while Sloan and Crosby stood to one side and Burns busied himself with some wire and arc lamps.

"Ah," said the pathologist again. "And not clothed in white samite either."

"Grey suiting," said Sloan automatically.

"So I see."

"Not a lot to go on, I'm afraid, Doctor. Just an arm."

"Oh, I don't know," said the pathologist easily. "I've had less in my time."

"This arm . . ." began Sloan. Once started on his

bizarre reminiscences there was never any stopping the Doctor.

"Had just an ear once," Dabbe said.

"On its own?" asked Crosby, clearly fascinated.

"Lonely as a cloud," said Dabbe poetically.

"This arm, Doctor," interrupted Sloan more firmly. He wasn't interested in unattached ears.

"This ear was . . ."

They were spared more by a light springing to life. While they had all been talking the ever-silent Burns, the doctor's assistant, had rigged up a powerful spot lamp and focussed it on the protruding arm. It more than made up for the missing light bulb. As soon as it was ready the pathologist—diverted from his ear story—applied his eye to the partially open door and gave the arm a long, long look.

"It's hairy, Sloan, so it's not a Chinaman."

"No, Doctor." That was the least of Sloan's worries.

"It's probably male all right."

Sloan hadn't been worried about that at all.

Dabbe grinned. " 'The apparel oft proclaims the man,' eh, Sloan? Not any more, it doesn't. But the fourth finger is longer than the first."

"Yes, Doctor."

Out of the corner of his eye Sloan saw Crosby glance down at his own hands and register the surprised look at one who finds that a natural rule applies to oneself as well as to everyone else.

"He's no horny-handed son of the soil," went on the pathologist.

"I was afraid of that," said Sloan.

"But he's used his hands . . ."

"Yes."

"The interdigital muscles are well developed. Nails well kept . . ."

Dabbe altered his stance a fraction. "No signs of disease manifesting itself in the hand—no clubbing of the fingers, no concave fingernails. No nicotine stains . . ."

Sloan made a note of that.

"And he didn't spend yesterday sun-bathing. In fact, I'd say he spent more time indoors than outside."

That would fit.

"No rings, wristwatch, or scars," the pathologist continued his observations. "A good tailor but an old suit," he added for good measure. "One button missing from the cuff."

"We know all about that."

"You do, do you? Your province, of course." Dabbe grunted and peered more closely still. "Can't tell you his exact age yet. The subcutaneous fat has started to go from the back of his hand. The skin doesn't look as if it's got the elasticity it used to have either." He paused. "Let's say not old, not young . . ."

"That would fit, too," said Sloan.

Dabbe straightened his bent back. "And you won't be unbearably surprised to know, Sloan, that he wasn't a mental defective either. As far as I can see from this side there are the regulation number of lines on his palm."

"Quite so," murmured Sloan. He could see Crosby glancing down at his own hands again. He wondered what comfort he would find there.

"Cause of death," continued the pathologist in a businesslike manner, "not immediately apparent. Crush injuries, I suppose, but in this job you never can tell."

"No, Doctor." Sloan was with him there: every inch of the way. The marble looked enough to kill anyone, but you never could tell.

Dr Dabbe took a last look through the narrow slit of open door and then straightened up again.

"A classic case, you might say, Sloan, of Death, the Great Leveller."

I SAW HIM EVEN NOW GOING
THE WAY OF ALL FLESH.

◆

7

There was something teasing about talking to a total
stranger on the telephone. A man's voice didn't tell anything like as much as did his appearance and his actions.
Sloan had never even spoken to the writer of the
anonymous letters over at the village of Constance Parva
but he would stake his pension that the holder of the
pen would be thin and angular; spiky and mean of spirit.

Henry Pysden just sounded cautious.

"He left here a little before six o'clock last evening,
Inspector. Like he usually did. We were naturally afraid
that something might be wrong when he didn't come in
this morning. Not like him at all . . ."

"There was a Mr Cranswick over at Cleete this morning, sir, who seems to have been expecting him to be there,
too."

"Ah," said Pysden regretfully, "I'm afraid I was rather
busy when he called here. On an important experiment
with a built-in time factor. On a refractory material. Sea-
water magnesia. I couldn't leave it and he wouldn't wait."

"I wanted to ask you about your work," said Sloan.
"What do Struthers and Tindall do?"

Pysden hesitated. "What we do is rather difficult to
describe, and we are—er—ah—um—a little—what shall
I say?—er—reticent about the exact nature of our work."

59

"Any confidence will, of course, he respected as far as possible," murmured Sloan diplomatically, "but we must know."

"Quite. Quite. I see that." The voice at the other end of the telephone line suddenly hurried into speech. "Shall we say—to put it in a nutshell . . ."

"Yes, sir?" Sloan was all in favour of that.

Always.

"I think Mr Tindall would not mind my telling you that what we do is other people's research and development for them."

Sloan wrote that down.

"Only in certain fields, naturally, Inspector. Now, about Mr Tindall . . ."

"Research and development, sir. Should I know what that means?"

The voice relaxed a little. "Not really, I suppose. No reason why you should. Research and development—R and D, it's usually called—is carried out by nearly all big firms these days. Mostly to make sure they'll have marketable products in five years' time."

"I see, sir."

It was different in the police force.

Market trends in crime changed, of course. One sort of mischief often surged to the forefront—became fashionable, you might say—while another receded for a while. But down at the Police Station they weren't troubled by the thought of running out of work five years hence.

In any number of years, come to that.

Short of the politicians finding Utopia, of course.

Or the scientists discovering a cure for Original Sin.

Or—more probably—the millennium arriving on the doorstep of the Home Office, so to speak.

Sloan didn't think that was likely either.

Henry Pysden was still talking. He'd got an unaccented voice, a bit on the reedy side.

"The work we do can amount to almost anything, of course, but firms usually stick to their own line. So that they can use their existing plant if possible. Saves re-tooling—that does cost a lot of money."

"And where exactly do Struthers and Tindall come in, sir?"

"Struthers and Tindall come in, Inspector, where you have a firm which doesn't have its own research and development department." He coughed. "Where one of these firms needs some specific work done—say when they've got a good idea and no facilities for following it through—then we do it for them. Or . . ." the reedy voice stopped.

"Or?" prompted Sloan.

Henry Pysden hesitated again. "Or when it has something very secret indeed which it wants an opinion on."

"Even," asked Sloan, anxious to get at least one thing in the case quite clear, "when it has a research and development department of its own?"

"Sometimes."

"Why?"

"A lot of reasons," said Pysden carefully. "They may have someone in their own firm whom they are—er—ah —um—not absolutely sure about . . ."

Sloan groaned inwardly. That was a point tailor-made for any policeman to take. Even Detective Constable Crosby should be able to pick that one up for himself.

"Or they may feel," went on the cautious voice at the Berebury end, "shall we say they may have reason to fear—that their own internal security isn't too good. Then they would use us instead . . ."

That, decided Sloan, was going to be a great help, that was.

"Inspector, there is just one thing at this end . . ."

"Oh?"

"We're a little bit concerned about one of our confidential reports."

"Yes?"

"One of our highly confidential reports." With emphasis.

"What about it, Mr Pysden?"

"We can't find it."

Miss Hilda Holroyd might not have wanted the police sent for in the first place. As the morning wore on, though, she positively began to look forward to their arrival.

She was having a trying time.

Besides having had Mr Tindall's visitor—Mr Gordon Cranswick—darting in and out like an urgent gadfly—there was her usual work piling up. She had already postponed the rest of Mr Tindall's appointments for the morning.

"Urgent personal and domestic reasons," she lied gallantly into the telephone, promising to ring back later.

She had also parried the Head of the Testing Department, who had technical problems; fended off young Mr Blake, who didn't seem to have enough to do; dispatched two optimistic young salesmen who wanted Struthers and Tindall to buy brand-new equipment which would halve their expenses—or so they said; and—probably most important of all—successfully placated the office cleaner and tea lady.

"Report?" Mrs Perkins was indignant. "I haven't seen no report." She was a small wiry woman with the vigour of ten. She advanced down the corridor, broom rampant. "And I haven't touched it neither."

"We've misplaced it, you see, Mrs Perkins."

Grudgingly. "What's it look like?"

"Green," said Miss Holroyd. "It's a green file."

Mrs Perkins sniffed. "I never touch nothing with writing on it."

"There would just be a number on the outside, that's all."

"That's writing, isn't it?" said Mrs Perkins incontrovertibly.

"We had it yesterday." Miss Holroyd did her best to sound soothing. "It's rather an important one . . ."

"Well, it wasn't nothing to do with me." Mrs Perkins rammed the broom on the floor with quite unnecessary force. "But if I should 'appen to see it . . ."

"Thank you."

"I done Mr Pysden," said the cleaner obliquely.

"Good," responded Miss Holroyd warmly, bearing in mind that while clever young scientists could be recruited with ease cleaners as reliable as Mrs Perkins were thin on the ground.

"Not that he noticed." Mrs Perkins sniffed. "He was that stuck in his experiment. If you was to say to him had I bin in I bet you he wouldn't know one way or the other. Not Mr Pysden."

"Oh, Mrs Perkins, surely not."

"Head that buried in his papers," declared Mrs Perkins, "you wouldn't credit it. Not like young Mr Blake. I should like to know when he gets any work done."

"I'm sure," interjected Miss Holroyd swiftly, "that Mr Pysden's room is all beautifully neat and clean since you've been in there, anyway."

"Well," Mrs Perkins seemed faintly mollified, "it's better than it was. I will say that." She brought her broom to attention at the perpendicular and said grandly: "If I should happen to see this green file which you've lost I'll let you know . . ."

But not even the argus-eyed Mrs Perkins could locate the United Mellemetics file anywhere in the works of Messrs Struthers and Tindall.

Miss Holroyd and Mr Pysden met again about this.

"It would have to be the United Mellemetics report," said Henry Pysden gloomily. "Of all the people I'd rather not have to tell, Sir Digby Wellow comes pretty near the top of the list."

Miss Holroyd was sympathetic. Sir Digby Wellow was one of the country's more colourful industrialists. And vocal to disaster-point.

"Was it," she ventured, "going to be a favourable report?"

"No, it was not," said Henry Pysden. "That's what's so worrying. Sir Digby sent it to us because he thought there might be something funny going on in United Mellemetics." He adjusted his glasses. "And according to Mr Tindall he wasn't wrong."

"Oh, dear."

"It's all very awkward, Miss Holroyd."

"We've never—er—misplaced a report before," she said. "You don't think—possibly—just this once—Mr Tindall took it home with him?"

"Perhaps. Not like him, though. He's never done it before. And it's against all the rules."

Miss Holroyd sighed. "It would be the one day when

he isn't here to ask. I don't quite know what we should do next."

"I do," said Henry Pysden grimly. "Get me United Mellemetics on the phone at Luston. A personal call to Sir Digby Wellow, please, Miss Holroyd."

It was a full minute after the workmen had finished welding before those watching it could see anything at all. The inimical glare of the fierce heat had stained the vision of everyone in the church who wasn't wearing goggles.

"Here she comes, mate."

"Easy there."

"Watch your end, Joe."

Joe apparently watched his end all right for—very slowly—the great oak door leading into the tower from the church started to move. Willing hands caught it and laid it down in the nave. A small shower of broken marble came spattering down with it.

Sloan stood well to one side, just looking.

So did the pathologist, Dr Dabbe.

The workmen trudged up and down the nave, seeing that the big door was safe where it lay. Already, in the way of optical illusions, it looked too big for the hole that it had left behind it. "Not so deep as a well, not so wide as a church door," thought Sloan involuntarily. Now where had that saying come from? His mother, probably. She was a great one for old sayings.

"What do you want doing now, guv'nor?"

"Nothing, thank you," said Sloan, his eyes once more rivetted on the arm. The solitary arm exhibited a dreadful fascination. It was thrust out through the debris for all the world like that of a drowning swimmer calling for help.

The welders looked relieved and trundled their oxygen and acetylene cylinders away. Sloan beckoned with his finger and Dyson, the official police photographer, and his assistant, Williams, both moved forward, cameras at the ready.

"A nasty accident?" enquired Dyson cheerfully. None

of the pictures which Dyson took so professionally was ever pretty, but he didn't let the fact get him down.

"A nasty incident," Sloan corrected him.

Dyson nodded and took his first picture. After the penetrating flame of the welding plant the flash of his camera's bulb seemed tame stuff indeed. He jerked his thumb. "How did Fred get under that little lot?"

"Richard," responded Sloan automatically. "His name's Richard."

He was more than ever sure now that it was.

"I don't suppose," remarked Dyson, who was an incorrigible looker on the bright side, "he knew what hit him. Can't have done."

"No. Now, what I want," said Sloan, getting down to business, "are a couple of shots of the height of the marble piled up against the outside door over there. That one . . ."

"The west door?" Dyson obediently started to focus.

"The coffin door," supplied Dr Dabbe ghoulishly from the sidelines.

The camera clicked, recording the marble heaped up against the door.

"Now what?" asked Dyson.

"I want some of that window up there. The little one above the door," said Sloan, "from the inside and the outside."

"No one could get through that, Inspector."

"No," agreed Sloan, "but it's been opened and the ladder taken outside to do it with, I daresay."

Dyson obligingly hitched his camera up and photographed the little window, while his assistant, Williams, rigged up a tripod in the nave.

"Been reading Sherlock Holmes, then, have you, Inspector?" he asked with a deceptively straight face.

"No," said Sloan shortly. "I haven't. Why?"

The photographer pointed up at the tiny window.

"It's a bit like in *The Speckled Band,* isn't it? No one could get through that window there, could they, and both doors were bunged up to the eyebrows with marble, so nobody could get out through them either."

"We'd got as far as that," said Sloan, though he

wasn't sure if Crosby had actually worked that much out yet . . .

"But something knocked that thing down on the poor chap and then vamoosed somehow. Stands to reason, doesn't it?"

"If," promised Sloan, "it turns out to have been a deadly Indian swamp adder, I'll let you know."

It was common knowledge in the Force that Dyson would have gone a long way on the uniform side if only he'd had the sense to keep his mouth shut at the right moment. Perhaps that was better, though, than Crosby who didn't seem to have opened his sensibly at all so far.

"Unless he went upwards," continued the police photographer logically, taking some pictures of the narrow stairway—more of a catwalk really—which climbed up round the tower and was lost to sight somewhere among the bells.

"If he went up that way," said Sloan, following his gaze, "I should like to know how he got down afterwards. It's too high for a ladder and it's a long drop without one. I don't know how you get back to earth from that sort of height . . ."

"Rapunzal," suggested Dr Dabbe, who was still waiting on the sidelines to be able to examine the dead man.

"Batman," offered Crosby, suddenly coming to life at last.

Sloan took a deep breath. He couldn't very well bawl Crosby out; not if the doctor was making dotty suggestions, too.

"Rapunzal?" he said, injecting the word with just enough of a note of polite enquiry as not to jeopardise the traditionally good relations between police and medicine.

"In reverse, of course," explained the pathologist. "You remember, Sloan, she was a maiden who was shut up in a tower by her father."

"Really, sir?" It sounded quite a good idea to him. If more fathers shut up their maiden daughters in towers more often there would be a lot less work and worry for some members of the police force.

"She grew her hair long," added the doctor, "and a knight in shining armour climbed up it."

Sloan choked.

"Grimm's Fairy Tales," said Dr Dabbe gravely.

"With Batman . . ." began Crosby.

Sloan rounded on him. "If that's your only suggestion, Constable . . ."

He stopped and gritted his teeth. Was this what was called the Generation Gap? The difference between Rapunzal and Batman?

He stopped because it wouldn't be any good saying anything.

He knew that.

He sighed. He would just have to have more help, that was all.

Real help.

Not just Constable Crosby standing two paces behind him, looking bored and making absurd suggestions, and a police photographer who was a detective *manqué*.

"This lady who let her hair down," said Dyson interestedly.

"If you've quite finished photographing that stairway, Dyson," snapped Sloan, "Crosby here can start getting it checked for footprints. Just in case."

It would be a waste of time. Sloan could see that from where he was standing. The treads were too clean. Either someone had deliberately dusted them down or they were kept that way.

By whoever wound the church clock, perhaps?

He could hear the machinations of the clock overhead as it gathered strength to strike the quarter hour above them.

There were some more flashes and then Dyson stood back and said: "That's the lot inside, Inspector. I'll come back and take a few bird's-eye views from up top when you've finished with the stairway."

Sloan nodded and exchanged glances with the pathologist, by now gloved and gowned.

There was a sudden change of mood inside the church tower as Dr Dabbe advanced, totally absorbed now in the arm.

They started to wade through the piled marble towards it. There was some writing on a piece of marble at Sloan's feet. He looked down and read it. *"Defunctae . . ."*

He must have said it aloud because the pathologist, who had at last reached the arm, said, "So's our chap, I'm afraid. Very."

◆

8

The Dower House at Cleete was no more empty now than it had been half an hour ago. There were exactly three people in it. The same number and the same people as there had been before. Fenella herself, Mrs Turvey, and Police Constable Hepple.

It was true that the Constable had gone through into the kitchen to talk to Mrs Turvey, but the complement of people within the house was still the same.

But it felt emptier.

Somehow her father's presence seemed to have left it.

Fenella hadn't quite grasped all that Police Constable Hepple had tried to tell her. Her ears had heard all right —there was no avoiding his slow, burred Calleshire speech—but her bemused and bewildered mind somehow hadn't picked up the messages from her ear. Her brain was a confused jumble of disconnected words— sculpture—crushed—arm—button—church.

If she had been seven years old again and at a children's party—not the sort of children's party which children had nowadays but the sort of children's party which they still had when she was a little girl—then the whole of Hepple's ghastly rigmarole could have been resolved in a hilarious game of consequences.

Sculpture—crushed—arm—button—church.

Someone in turn would then have added the ultimate

69

incongruity—father. Then there would have been shrieks of laughter and everyone would have gone on to the next game. Or a kind, motherly hostess would have handed out lemonade all round.

She sat quite still.

This was no game.

And there wasn't going to be any laughter.

Not now.

Not for a long time.

She could have done with the lemonade though. Her mouth was dry and she seemed to have too much tongue. There would be some tea coming soon. The Constable had said so. That was what he had gone through into the kitchen for.

A cup of tea.

The police panacea.

And to tell Mrs Turvey about her father. That was nice of him. She hadn't wanted to—didn't feel she could —start on about the sculpture and the arm and the button to Mrs Turvey just now.

At least Mr Gordon Cranswick of Cranswick (Processing) Limited or whatever it was would know now why it was that her father couldn't see him this morning. She had known—she knew—he wasn't a breaker of promises . . . not her father.

It was because Police Constable Hepple was in the kitchen that Fenella Tindall got to the telephone first. She picked it up automatically without thinking almost as soon as it started to ring.

A deep male voice asked for Richard Tindall.

"He's not here," she said falteringly. "Who is this?"

"Where is he, then?"

"Who is this speaking?" countered Fenella.

"Wellow," boomed a voice that was practically basso profundo. "Digby Wellow of United Mellemetics of Luston."

"Oh . . ."

"I require to speak to him," announced the caller magisterially, "as soon as possible."

"I'm afraid you can't."

"Why not?"

"Something's happened," she said helplessly. "Something terrible's happened."

"What?" howled a suddenly anguished voice at the other end of the line. "Tell me . . ."

But this was something that Fenella found she could not do. She stood by the telephone, her mouth working soundlessly, tears beginning to chase themselves quietly down her cheeks as she attempted to convert tragedy into words. She was making the painful discovery—as many another before her—that to comprehend bad news was one thing: to convey it to someone else quite another. Perhaps it was because to formulate the words might somehow seem to endorse the very worst . . .

This was where the kindly Hepple found her when he came back with a cup of tea a minute or so later. He lifted the telephone receiver from her nerveless fingers, listened intently for a moment, heard nothing but the dialling tone, and then replaced it.

When Paul Blake rang from Struthers and Tindall's offices a few minutes later to speak to Fenella, Police Constable Hepple answered the call himself.

In the church tower they—Dr Dabbe and his assistant, Burns, Inspector Sloan, and Constable Crosby—began uncovering the body attached to the visible arm. It was a slow, painstaking business, each piece of marble being marked and then laid in the aisle. Little by little a crumpled figure began to emerge from under the debris of the Fitton Bequest.

Incredibly, the operation was not without its lighter moments.

"Is this an angel, Inspector?"

Sloan looked up. Crosby was cradling a curvaceous marble infant, undamaged save that it lacked an arm. Its other arm—chubby to a degree—seemed to be toying playfully with the detective constable's lapel.

Sloan gave a sigh of pure exasperation.

Crosby gave the marble a friendly pat. "Or is it a cherub, sir?"

"Neither," said Sloan shortly. "It's one of the ten Fitton children. Now, give me a hand with this bit, will you? It's too heavy for one."

In fact, it took all four of them to lift the largest piece of all from the top of the body on the floor.

"Multiple fractures, for a start," decided Dr Dabbe, who had reached his quarry at last. "And a ruptured spleen, I should say."

Sloan waited. To him the man just looked like a rag doll with the stuffing gone.

"She's broken his back, all right, too," announced the pathologist a moment or two later.

"Who has?" asked Sloan considerably startled.

"The widow."

"Oh." His brow cleared. "Mrs Fitton."

The doctor bent over the body again and Sloan had time to take his first good look round the inside of the tower itself.

It was a very high one and open right up to the bells. He could just make them out in the dimness some seventy feet above his head. Sundry ropes hung down from the bell loft. Those from the bells were neatly moored against the wall opposite where the sculpture had been parked on its plinth. A single rope secured them to the wall near a brass plaque.

Sloan picked his way across the floor to read the inscription.

"To call the folk to Church in time,

                     WE CHIME

When joy and pleasure are on the wing,

                     WE RING

When the body parts the Soul,

                     WE TOLL."

"Nice, that, sir, isn't it?" said Crosby over his shoulder.

"He could have rung one of the bells," said Sloan, looking back to the body, "if he thought there was any danger. There was nothing to stop him doing that."

Crosby said, "So he wasn't worried, sir."

"Not about the Fitton Bequest, anyway."

"He could have walked out, too," added Crosby, "if he hadn't been happy. The tower door wasn't locked, was it, sir?"

"Between eleven last night and eight this morning it was."

"We don't know," said Crosby going off on a fresh tack, "why he came here either."

"There's a lot we don't know," Sloan reminded him with gloomy relish, "yet."

The pathologist straightened up from the prone body. "There's one thing we do know, Sloan . . ."

"Yes, Doctor?"

"He was hit twice."

"Twice?"

"Once to make him unconscious, the second time by all the marble. That's what killed him. He didn't bleed after that."

"How do you . . ."

"He bled the first time," said the doctor succinctly. "He was lying on his face then. You can see how the blood trickled down the sides of his head and dried there. Some of it dropped on the ground from his head. I can confirm that for you presently . . ."

Crosby's head came up in a challenging fashion.

". . . from the shape of the drop," said the pathologist, answering the unspoken gesture. "If it's a short distance then you can work it out. The shape of the drop varies with the height it has fallen."

"Then?" said Sloan hastily.

"Then the marble came down on top of him. After that, Sloan, all the King's Horses and all the King's Men couldn't have put him together again."

"How much later?" Why was it that fairy tales and nursery rhymes were all so sinister? Tales for children. Tales you brought children up on. Never mind the violence they saw on television later on.

"Good question." The pathologist waved an arm. "I'll see what I can do for you there. He was hit from behind the first time and from above the second. No doubt about that." Dr Dabbe stooped and lifted the last of the marble —a small chip—from the back of the dead man's neck and murmured, "Pelium upon Ossa."

Burns gave a short sharp laugh, rather like a seal barking.

Sloan, who was never sure about the doctor's medical jokes, turned his attention back to the tower wall.

It was unexceptional enough. Beside the bell ropes were various little framed cards commemorating past bell-ringing triumphs—marathon rings of Double Norwich Court Bob Major and Treble Bob Maximus. Above them a dark, time-stained board recorded some ancient parish charity.

There was no message scratched on any of the walls that Sloan could see. If the tower had been a temporary prison Richard Tindall did not seem to have appreciated the fact to the extent of writing on the walls.

Nor was there anything remotely resembling a weapon.

He said so.

"Ha," remarked the pathologist neatly, "if not malice aforethought then malice afterthought."

Sloan translated this for Crosby's benefit. "Whoever hit him took away whatever they hit him with."

Dabbe considered the man's head. "Something blunt and not very big, Sloan. That's what you should be looking for."

Crosby, in fact, wasn't paying attention anyway. He had found a small mirror and, stooping, was regarding himself in it.

"If, Constable," remarked Sloan nastily, "it's a question of who is the fairest of us all . . ." Now he was catching the nursery rhyme habit, too.

"They've hung it a bit low, sir," complained Crosby.

"Spotty choirboy height," said Dr Dabbe without looking up. He never missed anything, did the doctor. "Now, Sloan, about the time of death . . ."

The pathologist looked at his watch. Driven by an inner compulsion which comes over everyone who sees someone else look at a watch, Sloan looked at his, too. It was almost eleven o'clock. The time struck a faint chord in his memory. Eleven o'clock. Now why had eleven o'clock mattered today?

The Mayor.

That was it. The Mayor was due to leave the Town Hall at eleven o'clock this morning. To do something or other that had seemed important to him, if not to the police force. Sloan tried to visualise the message he had seen for only a brief moment before he had hurried out to Cleete. It wasn't the Flower Show. He knew that was next Saturday all right because of holding Princess Grace back. If it wasn't the Flower Show, what could it have been . . .

It came to him.

The Water Works.

The Mayor had been due to leave for the new Water Works at eleven o'clock this morning to declare it open and cut a ribbon or turn on a tap or something. Well, the Mayor would have to take his chance at the Water Works today.

"Just over the twelve hours, I should say," the pathologist broke into his thoughts. "Give or take an hour or so either way. I might even be able to calculate the interval between the two blows. I'll get nearer the time for you later on anyway when I've done the post-mortem. Brain tissue's all the thing for timing these days."

"That won't be difficult to get," offered Crosby.

"We think," intervened Sloan swiftly, "we know where he was yesterday evening—if his daughter's telling the truth, and if he's Richard Tindall, of course."

"Not my department, old chap, his name." Dr Dabbe started to take his gown off. "The post-mortem'll tell you practically everything else about the poor fellow—no secrets there—but not his name. Not yet. I expect we'll come to it in time. When babies are branded at birth with a computer number, God help us all." He tossed his gown over to Burns. "I'm finished here now, Sloan. Done all I can. It's all yours . . ."

Sloan didn't need telling. He looked round for Crosby. The constable had waded across to look at the plinth. "Crosby, what . . ."

"I've found some more Fitton girls over here, sir. On the four corners of the plinth. They're a bit more grown-up than the others."

"I wish you were," said Sloan, much-tried. "Try reading the small print."

"Oh, I see, sir." Crosby looked more closely and then slowly spelled out: "Temperance, Prudence, Justice . . . I can't quite get round to this one . . . oh, yes . . . Fortitude."

"The four cardinal virtues," said Dr Dabbe, who had been well brought up.

"You wouldn't know about them, Crosby," said Sloan unkindly.

Dr Dabbe mentioned a cardinal virtue which the late Mr Fitton, father of ten, did not seem to have possessed but Constable Crosby had by now seen something else. He bent down towards the bottom of the back of the heavy marble slab and pointed.

"The plinth," said Dr Dabbe in a suddenly cold voice. "Look down there, Sloan."

Sloan moved forward so that he could see.

"At the back," said the pathologist.

"Wedges," said Sloan. "Iron wedges. Proper ones."

He promptly dispatched Crosby to check with Bert Booth, the foreman, whether the workmen had put the wedges there. Somehow he didn't think they had.

"To tilt it forward?" suggested Dabbe.

"But not too much."

"Just so far . . ."

"That something could knock the sculpture off easily . . ." concluded Sloan grimly.

"But what?"

A complete search of the floor of the tower, scrupulously conducted, produced only broken marble and a spent match. The match was under a piece of marble just inside the west door and beneath the little slit window.

Sloan felt it wasn't a lot to go on.

◆

9

"Well?" barked Superintendent Leeyes down the telephone.

"It's Richard Tindall, all right, sir."

"All right is scarcely the phrase, Sloan."

"No, sir. Sorry, sir."

"Well?" he barked again.

"We're doing what we can," Sloan assured him hastily,
"but there were all those marble bodies lying in the . . ."

"Sounds like a knacker's yard," said Leeyes more
cheerfully.

"Yes, sir," said Sloan evenly. It was all right for the
Superintendent sitting safely in his office in Berebury. He
hadn't had to hump the marble about. The Superintendent—like Hamlet—had risen above action.

"Who benefits?" Superintendent Leeyes's view of police
life was in its way every bit as simplified as Crosby's.

"I don't know, sir, yet." He cleared his throat. "There's
a lot we don't know."

He'd said that to Crosby, too.

"The great thing," declared Superintendent Leeyes, "is
to state your problem."

He had once been on a Management Course and had
returned permanently confused about aims and objects.

"Yes, sir."

"In as few words as possible."

77

"Yes, sir."

"So that you know that you're doing and why."

Goals, they had called them on the course, but he had forgotten that.

"Yes, sir."

"Well," he growled, "what's your problem?"

"How the Fitton Bequest got on top of Tindall," said Sloan promptly.

There was a long pause. Then:

"No booby traps over the door, Sloan?"

"No, sir. I checked."

"Nothing attached to the clock?"

"Not even a cuckoo, sir."

A voice said icily as if from a great distance, "You know perfectly well what I mean, Sloan. When the hands reached—say—midnight they could have triggered something off . . ."

For one delicious moment Sloan dallied with the idea of mentioning Cinderella too; but decided against it. He had his pension to think of.

"There was no sign of anything, sir," he said instead.

There had been no sign of anything at all out of the ordinary about the tower. As church towers went it had seemed to Sloan like all the other church towers he had ever known: a square of ancient architecture with an assortment of dangling bell ropes in the middle.

"What about a detonator under the sculpture, Sloan? Had you thought of that?"

"Yes, sir. We looked for signs of explosive devices. Burn marks, and so forth . . ." The Superintendent never gave up. You had to say that for him.

Leeyes grunted. "And nothing to actually prove that the blasted thing hadn't just slipped, either, I suppose . . ."

"The gang who moved it," replied Sloan carefully, "can't remember putting any wedges underneath it at all. They swore it was steady enough when they left it—but then they're not going to say anything else, sir, are they?"

"Not if they know what's good for them," growled Leeyes, who was nothing if not a realist where the British workman was concerned. "Not now . . ."

"No, sir. Not now . . ."

"So what have we got, Sloan, that's any good to us?"

"One," enumerated Sloan, "a dead man, who may be Richard Tindall; two, a missing report, which may or may not be important; three, some tale about the firm being sold yesterday to a man who's been and gone again . . ."

"And?"

"Some scuff marks on the gravel outside the embrasure window."

"Anything else?"

"A ladder out of place. It wasn't in the church tower where it was usually kept. It was lying outside, and round the corner."

"That all?"

"There was a used match on the floor of the tower which may or may not have anything to do with the case."

"You'll have to do better than that, Sloan, for a jury."

"Yes, sir, I know."

"And don't be too long about it. There's something else waiting for you when you get back."

"Sir?"

"A shoe. A woman's shoe. Size six. Part worn—just too much for discomfort, not enough to throw it away."

"Just the one?"

"Just the one," Leeyes said. "The left one. It's where they found it . . ."

"Canal bank?"

"Golf course," said that master of the Parthian shot.

Sloan groaned.

On his way back from using Mr Knight's telephone again, Detective Inspector Sloan turned aside and made his way past the church tower towards the little cottage opposite. He noticed as he went by that the scuffed gravel outside the west door had been covered over by Crosby. So had the ladder which Bert Booth had carried round from somewhere behind the tower. Not that Sloan was hopeful that the ladder would yield any helpful fingerprints. Fingerprints were for easy cases. Something told him this wasn't going to be an easy case.

His approach had been observed. He had hardly raised his hand to the knocker on the door of Vespers Cottage when it flew open.

"Yes?" said a small round woman with alacrity.

Behind her stood another small round woman.

Sloan explained himself.

So did they.

"I'm Miss Ivy Metford," said one.

"I'm Miss Mabel Metford," said the other.

"We're sisters," said Miss Ivy superfluously.

"Two unclaimed treasures," chimed in Miss Mabel.

"Quite so," said Sloan hastily. "I'm afraid . . . I fear that someone has been crushed . . ."

"An elm?" suggested Miss Ivy promptly.

"An elm?" echoed Sloan, bewildered. This was very nearly as difficult as talking to the Superintendent.

Miss Mabel waved a hand towards the churchyard behind him and intoned: "The elm hateth man and waiteth . . ."

"It wasn't an elm, madam."

"Not an elm." They nodded in unison.

Sloan pulled himself together. "What I want to know is if either of you saw anyone about here last night or early this morning."

Two heads shook as one.

"No one?"

"Just Mr Knight, of course."

"And Tessa."

"Tessa?"

"His dog."

"No one else?"

Miss Mabel cocked her head to one side. "There was a night fisher . . ."

"A night fisher?"

Miss Ivy explained quite kindly. "A man with a fishing rod going down to the river. About two o'clock in the morning, that was."

The aura of anxiety at the Dower House at Cleete had been succeeded by one of mourning. It was a house of stillness now. Hepple let Sloan and Crosby in by the back door.

"It's Mrs Turvey I want to talk to first," announced Sloan.

But the short stout daily woman in the Dower House kitchen could no more account for what had happened to Mr Tindall than could his daughter.

"Enemies? 'Course not. He wouldn't hurt a fly. Ever such a nice quiet gentleman, he was, Inspector. And no trouble to no one."

"Really?" commented Sloan, making a note.

Quietness might very well be a recommendation to a daily woman. It wasn't necessarily one to a policeman. The last very quiet gentleman with whom Sloan had had dealings had been a professional blackmailer.

He didn't suppose the anonymous letterwriter from the village of Constance Parva would be noisy, either.

Very quiet, Mrs Turvey said again, especially since the mistress died, but then that was only to be expected, wasn't it?

Sloan coughed discreetly and enquired if there were any signs that Mr Tindall had been—er—contemplating marrying again.

"None," declared Ada Turvey positively. "He was lonely. That's only natural. You could see that he was lonely with half an eye—anyone could—that's why Miss Fenella came back—but he never seemed interested in no one else. Not after the mistress."

"Or of—er—not marrying again—if you take my meaning?"

Mrs Turvey took it all right, and shook her head.

"What about worries?"

Mrs Turvey smoothed down her apron. "We've all got worries, haven't we?"

"Special worries . . ."

She shook her head again. "Not that I know of, Inspector. Just Miss Fenella."

"What about her?"

"He was worried if he was doing the right thing letting her come back from Italy just to look after him. That I do know. Didn't think it would be good for a young girl burying herself in the country on her own. What with her poor mother being gone and everything."

"I see."

"She would come home," said Mrs Turvey. "There was no stopping her. Very attached to her father she was."

"And to anyone else?" enquired Sloan. A girl like that wasn't going to lack admirers. "She told us she was out most of yesterday evening . . ."

"That was with an Italian friend. Giu . . . Giu . . . something Mardoni, he's called. Mr Mardoni, anyway. Someone she knew in Italy. Over here for a few days. Took her to that new Italian restaurant, he did, that's just opened. He was going straight back to Rome."

"When?"

"Last night. A night flight. Home by half-past ten easily, Miss Fenella said she was, so that this Mr Mardoni could get to the airport on time."

"Is there," enquired Sloan routinely, "anyone else besides this Italian friend?"

Mrs Turvey sniffed and said it wasn't for her to say but there was that Mr Blake.

"Mr Blake?"

"Paul Blake. He's one of the bright boys from the master's works. Practical scientist or some such thing he calls himself. Been making sheep's eyes at Miss Fenella, he has, ever since she came home."

Sloan made note of the name.

"If you ask me," said Mrs Turvey, sniffing again, "what that young man's got is an eye for the main chance."

Sloan nodded. That wouldn't surprise him at all. Of all the manifold rules for success in this world one stood out head and shoulders above all the others.

Marrying the boss's daughter.

And the good books didn't even mention it.

He cleared his throat. "What did Mr Tindall think?"

"I reckon he wasn't keen," responded Mrs Turvey promptly, "but he's got too much sense to try to stop Miss Fenella."

"Not easily stopped?" hazarded Sloan, thinking of a pair of clear eyes and finely moulded chin.

"She's got a mind of her own," admitted the daily woman.

"Mr Tindall had no other problems that you were aware of?" asked Sloan formally. Daughters were, after all, the normal worries of normal fathers. They didn't usually drive the fathers to leave home.

On the contrary, in fact ...

"Mardoni," repeated Superintendent Leeyes after him, spelling it out. "Signor Giuseppe Mardoni, a passenger back to Rome late last night."

"Or very early this morning."

"I'll get them to start checking for you ..."

"Thank you, sir." Dutifully Detective Sloan radioed Berebury Police Station as soon as he had something—however crumblike—to report. Not that that would be soon enough for his superior officer.

"I've spoken to Mr Tindall's general manager, too, sir. A chap called Henry Pysden. He says everything's all right over at the works ..."

"Doesn't mean a thing."

"... except that they've lost this confidential report."

"They have, have they?"

"Belonging to United Mellemetics."

Leeyes grunted. "That's Sir Digby Wellow's little lot, isn't it? Over at Luston. The chap who can't keep his mouth shut."

If the highly paid and very professional Public Relations people retained by United Mellemetics to keep its name before the public could have heard this they would have swooned gently. They were very gentle men altogether.

Sloan, however, knew what he meant. He forged on.

"Otherwise, according to the daughter, it seems Mr Tindall spent yesterday quite normally. Nothing apparently out of the ordinary, anyway. And the business looks all right."

"Businesses," said Leeyes largely, "often look all right when they aren't."

"Yes, sir."

"What's his life-style like?" Leeyes wanted to know.

Sloan sighed. The Superintendent had never been the same since he had read a book on sociology.

"Er—good, sir."

He might have known it wasn't the right answer.

It never was with sociology.

"Try again, Sloan."

"A nice house," he said defensively, "and a big garden. All well kept."

"Ah," pronounced the Superintendent hortatively, "the carriage trade."

"Yes, sir," said Sloan, who considered this—after sociology—a most unfair lapse into an earlier idiom. "Exactly, sir."

"Anything else?"

"His car's at home," said Sloan carefully.

"He won't have walked to Randall's Bridge," pronounced Leeyes immediately. "Nobody walks anywhere these days. That's the whole trouble with our traffic system. Ask 'em to park a hundred yards away from where the little dears want to go and they won't do it."

Inspector Sloan sighed. Once he was truly astride, dismounting the Superintendent from a favourite hobbyhorse became a ticklish business.

"Mr Tindall's car's here, sir," he said firmly. "Standing in the garage but . . ."

"The whole race'll forget how to walk soon . . ." He was well in the saddle now.

"In the garage," repeated Sloan. It was reminiscent of a joust: tilting him off.

"That's just what I said, Sloan. He'll have gone by car wherever he went."

"We found him at Randall's Bridge, sir."

"Your trouble," retorted Leeyes robustly, "is that you aren't looking for clues in the right place. What you want to do," he added in atrocious French, "is to *cherchez la femme.*"

Sloan cleared his throat and said deliberately: "Whether Mr. Tindall put the car there himself or someone else put it there instead—well, I wouldn't like to have to say. Not at this stage."

"What's that, Sloan?"

"The car, sir."

"What about the car? I said to look for the lady."

"I have a feeling that Mr Tindall might not have brought it back to the garage himself."

"Why not?"

"There's a slight chip of paint off the driver's door—at the extreme edge—where it's been opened against the wall . . ."

"And?"

"And a tiny sliver of the same paint on the gardening tool which was hanging on the wall at the same level."

"Ha!"

"Yes, sir."

"The good old exchange principle." The Superintendent sounded almost gleeful over the telephone. "If objects meet they exchange traces. You can't beat it, can you?"

"No, sir." Dutifully.

"Fundamental, Sloan. The best rule in detection if it comes to that. And well over a hundred years old."

Sloan sighed. A hundred years wasn't going to be long enough to get his points over to the Superintendent.

Not at this rate.

"It looks to me, sir," he said firmly, "very much as if whoever brought that car into the garage last drove just a fraction too much to the right-hand side."

"Small garage?"

"Big car."

"Sloan are you trying to tell me he was abducted after all?"

"No, sir. Not that I know of."

"But this car was put there last night . . ."

"Perhaps we can't prove it was last night," admitted Sloan. "I don't know about that yet."

"Well, then . . ."

"Except that the car is in exactly the right place now for that chip to have happened last time the car door was opened."

"You can tell if you didn't put your own car away yourself," declared the Superintendent didactically. "Like you can tell if someone else has used your best fountain pen."

"Yes, sir," agreed Sloan, "but whether the daughter or the daily woman could tell that for us . . ."

Leeyes grunted.

". . . that's another matter," pointed out Sloan. "It isn't as if it was—er—their fountain pen, so to speak."

"Fingerprints?"

"Crosby's doing them now, sir, and then we're going round to Struthers and Tindall's works and to see these people Osborne who he spent the evening with." Sloan coughed. "Any sign of Mr Cranswick at your end, sir?"

"Not yet."

"Or the other shoe?"

"All that's comes in so far, Sloan, is another of those anonymous letters from Constance Parva. Someone's just brought it in. Between a pair of tongs . . ."

◆

10

Detective Constable Crosby had just finished going over Richard Tindall's car by the time Sloan got back to the Dower House garage.

"Well, what did you find?"

Crosby was good on cars, that was one good thing.

"Mr Tindall's prints all over the place, sir. Same as on that hairbrush Miss Tindall gave us for a sample. But . . ." he drew breath impressively.

"But what?"

"But on top of them there's a whole set of glove smudges. Sir, whoever drove this little outfit last wore gloves—that's for sure."

Sloan grunted.

"I've been over the lot," said Crosby. "Steering wheel, gear lever, keys, door handle, roof . . ."

"Roof?"

"You can't get out of a little number like this without putting your hand on the roof—just over the driver's door." Crosby moved forward eagerly. "Shall I show you, sir?"

"No," said Sloan sourly.

The exchange principle already invoked by the Superintendent applied to the driver and the car in the same way as to the car and the garage wall. Fourteen stone

of detective constable must also make their mark and
ruin any traces there might still be of the last occupant.

"You can't get any purchase unless you do, sir," persisted Crosby, "because of its being so low slung."

"I am not so old, Crosby," retorted Sloan, considerably
nettled, "that I have forgotten how to get out of a car
like this."

"No, sir. Of course not, sir. Sorry, sir." He began to
fumble for his main theme. "Otherwise, sir, there's just
this scrape of paint. It looks quite freshly damaged. I've
got a sample from the car and another from the edge of
the agricultural implement on the wall . . ."

"The what, Crosby?" Sloan mustered a little patience
from somewhere.

"Spade, sir."

"I should think so, indeed." The Superintendent could
call it what he liked but as far as constables were concerned spades were spades. If not shovels.

"I've got a couple of samples ready for the laboratory
people, sir." Crosby indicated two sealed packets. "They
can tell us for certain if they are one and the same
paint."

Sloan nodded.

He wasn't worried about the forensic chemist. The evidence was either for sure or so highly technical that the
jury believed it anyway. What he had to worry about
was police evidence—the evidence that juries did make
up their minds about—if they made their minds up on
evidence at all, that is—and there didn't seem to be a
lot of that about so far.

Just a dead man. Richard Mallory Tindall.

If he was Richard Tindall.

Even that wasn't absolutely certain yet.

He stood for a moment looking down at the long low
blue car. The position of the car might just be evidence.
He wasn't sure. His experience was that cars like this
were cherished by their owners—not carelessly chipped
against the wall. But a stranger not used to driving it who
was bringing it in to an unfamiliar garage on a dark night
might not have noticed that the spade was hanging there:
or misjudged the swinging arc of the really wide driver's
door of a two seater car.

It wasn't much to go on.

And he didn't like it particularly.

It smacked of a great deal too much forethought for his liking. Quick crime was one thing: this sort of calculation quite another.

He went back indoors and sought out Fenella Tindall.

"Now, miss, if you can spare me a minute . . ."

"Yes, Inspector?"

"Did your father drive in gloves?"

"Gloves? In all that heat?"

"Yes, gloves." Sloan knew some of these late-middle-aged fast car drivers. They wore special leather and string driving gloves and pretended all the time that they were young men at Le Mans.

The girl in the brown dress shook her head in a numbed way. "No, Inspector. Only in the winter. When it was very cold."

"Thank you, miss. That's what I thought."

"And not always then. He thought it was affected."

So did Sloan.

"There's something else we could do with, miss. The name and address of your Italian friend in Rome."

He shut his notebook after he'd written it down. "Now, I'm going over to your father's works, but I'll be back. Constable Hepple will stay here with you in the meantime. Is that all right?"

Fenella nodded dumbly.

The police car got them to the offices of Messrs Struthers and Tindall in Berebury at a more decorous speed than hithertofore. Detective Constable Crosby was still at the wheel but he was thinking.

"It's a funny business, sir, isn't it?"

"You can say that again."

"It looks as if he just stood there while someone hit him and then that ruddy great thing fell on him while he was lying there."

"There were no signs of a struggle," said Sloan, who had looked. "And no rope marks on his wrists or ankles. It looks as if he went there on his own accord, though we don't know why yet . . ."

"A bit of slap and tickle? 'Stop it, I like it' stuff ..."
suggested the Constable.

"In a church tower?" The Superintendent had said
cherchez la femme, too, hadn't he?

"Nice and quiet," said Crosby defensively.

Too quiet, thought Sloan. That was the whole trouble
with the church tower at Randall's Bridge. Even Vespers
Cottage was out of earshot.

"Perhaps," continued the Constable helpfully, "someone
sent him a note."

"I daresay they did."

"You know the sort of thing, sir," he elaborated.
" 'Meet me in the church tower at midnight.' Something
like that."

"Written in blood?" enquired Sloan genially. "And
finishing with 'Fail at your peril'?"

"That's right, sir." Crosby waved his hand in an eager
gesture.

"You'll have to stop watching all those bad films,"
pronounced his superior officer severely, though they
had funnier letters than that at the police station every
morning. "This isn't a Victorian melodrama."

"He was lured to his doom, all right, though, sir, wasn't
he?" intoned Crosby mournfully.

"Yes, but there's no need for keening," said Sloan
briskly. Perhaps it was more melodramatic than he
thought. "I should say he went to the church with somebody and what you've got to do is to check at ..."

It was too late. Crosby was already following yet
another train of thought.

" 'There was I,' " he mimicked in a pseudo-falsetto,
very high-pitched, " 'Waiting at the church ...' "

"Watch it," advised Sloan, "or they'll be having you
for the church choir. In with the boys."

Crosby went very quiet.

"There's another thing we don't know for sure,"—
Sloan went back to his brief—"and that's how the deceased got to the church tower."

"Car," said Crosby, who could never envisage any
other form of locomotion anyway.

"It was gone by eleven if it was. That schoolmaster
fellow—the one who knows all about everything ..."

"Mr Knight," supplied Crosby.

"Him. He didn't say anything about a car being parked by the church last night when he took his dog for a walk, did he? And he would have done, surely, if he'd seen it. A strange car would ring a bell. Especially a slap-up job like Tindall's . . ."

"Another car, then?"

"Or the deceased's car parked somewhere else. And gone by eleven. Before Knight came back that way with his dog."

Their own car was very nearly at Berebury's Wellgate now. Sloan could see Struthers and Tindall's works looming up.

"That's your next line of enquiry, Crosby. Was there any other car which could have been involved parked in Randall's Bridge last night. Or the deceased's. And while you're about it find out what time Tindall's car really left the Osbornes, and where it went after that if you can."

"Yes, sir."

"And what time it got back to Cleete."

"Yes, sir."

"The girl said some time after eleven but she may be wrong." That was something else he would have to go into presently: if Fenella Tindall was speaking the truth. "And time the distance from the Osbornes to Randall's Bridge."

"Yes, sir."

"And Crosby . . ."

"Sir?"

"Police time, not Crosby time."

"Yes, sir."

"Hepple will tell you who to talk to. He'll know who is likely to have been out and about in Cleete that late."

"Late, sir? Half-past ten?"

"That," rejoined Sloan neatly, "is why the country is called the hush. Didn't you know?"

As he stepped over the threshold of Messrs Struthers and Tindall's works Sloan decided one thing promptly enough. That if Superintendent Leeyes was right in saying *cherchez la femme* one thing was pretty certain:

that Mr Tindall's personal secretary wasn't the *femme*. Like most ugly women she didn't show her age. She had, however, a pleasant, rather deep voice.

She stood up as they introduced themselves.

"It's usually Inspector Tetley who comes over when we want anything. We just ring . . ."

"He's Crime Prevention," said Sloan, also a servant of the public. Fred Tetley dealt with Crime Prevention in Berebury Division and he was the only optimist on the entire strength. He was the officer who went round recommending bars here, bolts there, and alarm bells with everything.

And not one of these estimable precautions had stopped Richard Tindall from dying.

"Inspector, what news . . ." she broke off as a dark-haired good-looking young man in a white coat put his head round her office door. He was waving a sheaf of papers in his hand.

"Excuse me, Miss Holroyd, but I can't find Mr Tindall anywhere and I've got those heat storage results for him down from Testing now. I've just finished checking them through."

"They were wanted yesterday, Mr Blake," said the secretary reprovingly. "Mr Tindall was waiting for them."

"Sorry." Mr Blake looked contrite—but not very.

A really handsome young man, decided Sloan, doesn't get much practice in looking abashed.

"And," added Miss Holroyd, "Mr Pysden wants the Patent Register."

"Everyone always wants the Patent Register."

"What everyone wants," remarked Miss Holroyd astringently, "is the United Mellemetics file."

"Not guilty," the handsome young man waved an arm airily as he backed out of the door. "I did my bit on that days ago."

Miss Holroyd turned back to Sloan. "I'm sorry, Inspector. You were saying . . ."

That she took the bad news about Richard Tindall with no more than a catch of breath and sudden paling did not weigh too heavily with Sloan. Outward calm was deceptive. He'd learned that much long ago. She was probably one of those people who always took all news with outward calm as a matter of policy. Good secretaries were like that. She could have taught the Superintendent a thing or two. He always hit the roof . . .

Five hundred years ago and he'd have been one of those who hanged the messenger who brought the bad news as an automatic preliminary to getting down to business.

"I'd better take you straight to Mr Pysden," she said gravely as soon as Sloan had explained. "Poor Fenella. I—we were afraid that something must be wrong when he didn't come in as usual this morning—but not as wrong as this . . ."

Perhaps, decided Sloan with approval, she was one of those people who believed that the manner in which news was received made a difference to the quality of the news.

Perhaps it did.

Sloan didn't know.

He only knew that what had happened to Richard Tindall wasn't something which could very well be relegated to the Fourth Division in the news class, however carefully invested with the commonplace.

And that it wasn't exactly Ghent to Aix stuff either.

At least, he corrected himself, it was only good news for one person. If it was murder, that was.

"We'll need to know about Mr Tindall's yesterday, miss."

"Of course." She was the efficient secretary at once. "Let me see now . . ."

Richard Mallory Tindall's yesterday seen from his secretary's viewpoint emerged as apparently uneventful. He had come in a little late because of the road works, and stayed in his office until about half-past eleven doing his letters. And beginning to write a report.

"The United Mellemetics report?" Sloan wanted to know.

Miss Holroyd shook her head. "The one which Mr Pysden is working on. The Marling Contract."

"Then what?"

The rest of the morning he had spent seeing people.

"Seeing who, miss?" he asked patiently.

Miss Holroyd frowned. "Mr Pysden, of course. He

had his daily conference with him over coffee as usual. That's when Mr Pysden gave him the United Melle-metics report. The one we can't find."

"You didn't see what he did with it?"

"I wasn't there."

"Go on. Who else did Mr Tindall see?"

"Mr Blake. You've just seen him, Inspector. And then the Works Foreman. Someone from Testing . . . oh, and Mr Hardy. He looks after the Patents and the legal side. I think that was all. The rest of the time he was talking on the telephone. Then he went round the works."

Sloan jerked his head. "Anything else?"

This was any businessman's any morning of any working day.

"Not that I know of, Inspector."

"Then what?"

"At twelve he went out to lunch."

"Where?" asked Sloan, dead on cue. It had the quality of a catechism did this going through the meaning of everything with this quiet responsive woman.

"I don't know." She hesitated. "He didn't say."

"Does . . . did he usually?"

She looked disconcerted. "As a rule."

"I expect we can find out easily enough, miss, if it turns out to be important. Anyone would remember that car of his . . ."

"He didn't take his car," she said flatly. "It stood out under my window all day."

"Someone called for him?" suggested Sloan.

"He took one of the firm's vans. The old runabout."

Sloan made a note of the number. Tracing it would give Crosby something useful to do when he had finished with the Osbornes: well, stop him from being underfoot for a bit anyway. "When did he get back?"

"He was here when I got back from lunch myself. Before two fifteen, anyway."

Sloan wrote that down, too. A man could go a fair way and back in a van in over two hours.

"And after lunch, miss?"

"More telephone calls."

"Including Mr Cranswick?"

Again a cloud passed over her face. "Not to my knowledge. Though,"—she pursed her lips—"he said he spoke to Mr Tindall yesterday. And that, Inspector, was about all he would tell me before he shot over to Cleete."

"We'd like to talk to him ourselves," said Sloan mildly. "We're looking for him now."

That was when the telephone rang.

It was Superintendent Leeyes to speak to Sloan.

"I've got something for you," said Leeyes. "You know this Italian chap who was with the daughter all yesterday evening . . ."

"Giuseppe Mardoni?"

"Him."

"What about him, sir?"

"He didn't catch his plane. We checked at the airport."

◆

11

"This way, Inspector . . ." Miss Holroyd led the way down a corridor towards another office. "Mr Pysden's in here . . ."

Sloan was conscious of the steady hum of power-driven machinery as soon as they stepped out of Miss Holroyd's office.

It was Henry Pysden to whom Sloan had spoken on the telephone from Cleete all right. His voice was still un-accented and reedy. He merged as a shortish middle-aged man with thick glasses.

"Poor Richard." He heard Sloan out and then took his glasses off and gave them a vigorous polish. "And poor Fenella. I never thought I'd see the day when I'd be glad Maisie was dead."

"Maisie?"

"His wife. In the church, did you say? What on earth was he doing there?"

"I couldn't say, sir." It was one of the many things Sloan would have to find out: and soon. He hadn't gone there to read the Lesson, that was one thing for sure. "Not at this stage," he finished formally aloud.

"Poor Richard," again. Pysden had obviously settled for the Book of Lamentations. "But Randall's Bridge wasn't even his church. Cleete was his parish, though I don't know that he was much of a churchman. Not," added Pysden hastily, "that he wasn't a good man. You wouldn't find a better, Inspector. And I should know. I've been with him a good many years. Longer than most people."

"No, sir, I'm sure." Sloan cleared his throat purposefully: the verbal obsequies would just have to wait. "You'll understand that we shall have to make extensive enquiries."

"Naturally."

"About him. And about your work here."

Pysden frowned. "I don't know that I'm in a position to tell you much about our work. Struthers and Tindall guarantee security, you know. And absolute secrecy. All part of our service. If anything at all leaks out we stand to cover the loss. I'm afraid," he added apologetically, "that we may have been somewhat of a burden to Inspector Tetley since we came here."

"All part of our service," murmured Sloan ironically.

"That's why people come to us who feel—who fear—who may have reason to fear—that their own security isn't too good."

"Like United Mellemetics?"

"Sir Digby Wellow is—er—most unhappy," said Pysden. "So are we. We've never had a—er—misplaced report before, have we, Miss Holroyd? Never."

"Never, Mr Pysden. Until now," she added conscientiously.

"I don't know what Richard will . . . oh, dear." Pysden took a deep breath. "Takes a bit of getting used to, doesn't it? That he's not going to be here to say it to . . ."

"Death's like that, sir. Now about this United Mellemetics report . . ."

"It was an important one." Pysden looked worried. "There was no doubt about that."

"Industrial espionage?" hazarded Sloan intelligently.

"It happens all the time." Pysden tacitly implied agreement and then turned to look at a large clock on the wall before peering myopically across at both police officers again. The thick lenses of his glasses somehow served to veil any expression on his face. If, thought Sloan obscurely, the eye was the window of the soul, like they said, then Henry Pysden's spectacles were a most effective curtain. "Bound to, really, Inspector, when you consider the sort of money involved these days in that size of firm."

"It makes a difference, sir." Sloan would like to see the situation in which money did not make a difference.

He hadn't yet.

"It was going to make a lot of difference at United Mellemetics anyway," said Pysden. "That's why Sir Digby came to us."

"He wasn't happy about something?"

"You could say that again." Pysden took a second look at the clock. "Either someone's judgement had gone haywire or there was some funny business going on over there. At least, that's what Richard told me yesterday. I don't know all the details myself. Mind you, it's not always as easy as you'd think to choose between the two. It's difficult to be entirely independent in your conclusions when the success or failure of your department in the firm rests on them. It could," he finished moderately, "be that."

It was a point of view, thought Sloan, which Inspector Harpe in Traffic Division would have appreciated. You never won in Traffic. And nobody ever had an independent view. Not if they drove a car, they didn't.

"Or," Pysden was going on, "it would be a case of every now and then a chap going to the opposite extreme and forgetting that commercial firms are not university research faculties. We get a bit of that."

So they did in the police force, too.

It drove them up the wall every three months or so.

Theorists, statisticians, psychologists, criminologists, penologists—they descended on the Berebury Police Station with monsoon regularity.

And were about as helpful.

"What firms usually want from us," said Pysden ponderously, "is the advance judgement of the marketplace. That comes into our work, of course. It must."

Sloan nodded. As far as he was concerned the judgement of the marketplace should come into a lot more things than it did.

Like a value-for-money prison system.

And traffic departments costed to within a life or two.

"But what Sir Digby wanted," said the deputy manager, "was an opinion on the work of an employee."

"Whether it was bad judgement or bad faith?"

"Precisely." Pysden let out his breath in a long sigh. "Precisely. It's always a bit tricky, you know, when it's someone in your own outfit who could be the—er—maverick. You've got to be really careful then."

They knew that in the Force without being told.

A rogue custodian was the biggest headache of all.

They said that the Chief Constable had something in Latin about that pinned over his shaving mirror. Someone who had stayed in his house had copied it out and the tag had gradually filtered down through the Force.

Quis custodiet ipsos custodes, it said.

One of the police cadets, fresh from school and a cocky little beast to boot, had translated it as "Who guards the guards."

"And which," Sloan asked the general manager, "was it, sir?"

"Bad faith, I'm afraid. At least," he qualified, "that's what Richard told me yesterday." There was no doubt that Pysden was watching the clock now. The hands were creeping round to half-past eleven. "I don't know all the details."

"You do work for other firms, too . . ."

"We do indeed."

"I shall need to know which ones, sir."

"And I shall need to have some authority before I give you their names, Inspector. It's all secret work, you know. Sometimes only the chairman of a particular firm knows that we're doing some work for them."

"Like United Mellemetics?"

"I very much doubt," said Pysden drily, "if Sir Digby has voiced his suspicions to anyone else . . ."

They were interrupted by a bell in the far corner of the laboratory. It rang from beside a complicated structure of wires, valves, glass, and metal. Henry Pysden immediately went straight across to it and took some readings from a thermometer and two little dials. He put these onto a graph and then punched a time recorder. A cylinder not unlike a barograph moved forward with a tiny jerk and Sloan could see that this was but the latest of a long series of recordings, all neatly time-punched.

"Sorry about this, Inspector," said Pysden over his shoulder, busy now with the apparatus, "but it won't wait. It's a time-linked experiment. I have to do this every six hours for a week . . ."

"Bad luck, sir."

Pysden grimaced. "All in a day's work, I suppose, except that the day starts on the early side. Half-past five."

"You have to get here by then?"

"No, no. I sleep here. There's a camp bed. What with the eleven thirty-one and the five thirty-one there'd be no night left if I didn't."

Pysden had his back to them now and was bending, totally absorbed, over something which looked to Sloan like a glass lathe.

"It looks very important, sir."

"It is, Inspector, believe me. I should say it's about the most important piece of work that Struthers and Tindall have ever done. It takes about twenty minutes each time and I can't delay it without ruining the whole experiment . . ."

"Of course, sir." Sloan got up to go.

"You'd better ask Fenella about the other business, Inspector. I daresay she comes into a controlling interest in Struthers and Tindall now . . ."

Detective Constable Crosby's lot had been to interview the Osbornes.

It had not been a happy one.

Bad news—a far fleeter traveller even than Crosby himself—had already reached chez Osborne. It was a neat and tidy dwelling, modestly prosperous, and set in a good residential area of Berebury near the park. Had Crosby been older and wiser he would have recognised one of those childless marriages where one partner doubles as a child. In this case it was the wife. A tearful Mrs Marcia Osborne was prostrate on a sofa. A kindly woman neighbour was in attendance trying to comfort her.

In vain.

"Poor Richard," Mrs Osborne kept on saying over and over again.

"There, there," adjured the neighbour ineffectually.

"Poor Richard," moaned Mrs Osborne.

Crosby stood well back from the sofa. Very well-dressed women frightened him enough even when they weren't crying: middle-aged women got up to look like girls terrified him at any time.

He wished there wasn't quite so much of Mrs Osborne's leg showing.

He wished he was back on the beat.

At least with a razor gang you did know where you were.

"I want George," cried Marcia Osborne.

Detective Constable Crosby, whose Christian name was William, felt quite relieved.

"Where's George?" she demanded.

The neighbour said, "I don't know, dear. It's the school dinner hour and they don't think he's in school."

"Why isn't he there?"

"I don't know, dear. The school secretary didn't say."

"He wasn't there at dinnertime yesterday either," said Marcia Osborne petulantly. "I want him. Now."

"Yes, dear." The neighbour—a resolute woman—having failed to administer psychological comfort or produce George Osborne in person conjured up something in a glass and commanded: "Drink this."

"Poor Richard," said Marcia Osborne mechanically, knocking back whatever it was in the glass with surprising swiftness. "He was here only last night. In that very chair."

Mesmerically all three of them stared at an empty chair next to the sofa.

"Last night . . ." began Crosby, knowing that he should be taking a proper interest in last night.

"Only last night," she echoed sorrowfully, turning to Crosby. "It doesn't seem possible, does it?"

"No, madam," said Crosby woodenly. "What time did he leave?"

Richard Tindall, it transpired damply, had left the

Osbornes' house at some point before half-past ten. Marcia Osborne was as vague about this as she was about the time he had arrived. About seven, she thought. At ten o'clock someone had rung for Tindall, and had asked to speak to him on the telephone. He had left shortly after that. No, she hadn't recognised the voice except that it was a man's. Business, was all Richard had said about it. Nothing more.

"He only had the tiniest drink before supper, too." She regarded Crosby between her tears. It was a predatory look.

Whatever the neighbour had given Marcia Osborne to drink it hadn't been tiny. She hiccuped slightly. Crosby noticed that the crow's-feet round her eyes gave a sympathetic ripple at the same time. It was as far as they could go considering the amount of make-up encasing them.

"And afterwards, madam?" He cleared his throat. "We are enquiring where everyone was last night."

She lowered her eyelashes. "In bed."

It shouldn't have been Crosby who blushed: but it was.

"Mr Tindall's visit was a social one, I take it, madam?"

Marcia Osborne turned her great limpid eyes towards him and opened them wide. "Why, no, officer. He came about George's invention. It's going to be a great success. Richard brought the good news last night." She gulped and started again "Poor Richard . . ."

Crosby fled.

Sloan had a list in his hand—prised out of the cautious Henry Pysden on Fenella's new-born authority—a list of Struthers and Tindall's customers.

What he hadn't got was any details of the United Mellemetics experiments.

Back in her office Miss Holroyd was explaining this.

"It's part of our system here, Inspector. We always gather up every single piece of paper to do with a client's experiments or project and return it to the customer with our report. That way we don't have any security problems with our old files. It's bad enough with the ones we're actually working on."

"Even scrap paper?" asked Sloan hopefully.

"Every last calculation—right or wrong—has to go back to them."

"What about the United Mellemetics report," Sloan enquired, clutching at a straw. "Who wrote that?"

"Nobody. At least," Miss Holroyd frowned, "I didn't and I usually type all the very confidential reports. Mr Tindall might have decided against a written report. He does sometimes."

"Why?"

Miss Holroyd sketched a gesture in the air. "Extra security, perhaps. We don't always give written reports anyway. They can be quite tricky, you know, in this line."

Sloan nodded gravely.

All policemen knew.

And they learnt it early.

In their line.

The hard way.

"Sometimes," explained the secretary, "Mr Tindall just talks to the people concerned. That way . . ." She hesitated.

"Yes?"

"A chairman can choose to use only what he wants of a particular verbal report. Bits here and there."

"No hard feelings, eh?"

"Exactly." She nodded. "And that way he can't be pressed for action either. Then or later."

"Clever."

"Chairmen of Companies," observed Miss Holroyd in a detached way, "usually are."

Sloan was with her there. Anyone could be a specialist. It was controlling the experts which ran you into trouble.

Miss Holroyd coughed. "There's another advantage, too, Inspector."

"Go on."

"Sometimes, when there's nothing in writing . . ."

"Yes?"

"The ideas and opinions we put forward can be made to seem to come from the Chairman himself."

"Not from Struthers and Tindall?"

"It has been known."

"The United Mellemetics Chairman—Sir Digby Wellow—is he one of those?"

"I should imagine," said Miss Hilda Holroyd delicately, "that a verbal report would have suited Sir Digby very well."

"But as far as you know he didn't have one?"

"No." She hesitated again. "He would be able to tell you that himself."

"He's not at United Mellemetics." Sloan pointed to the telephone on her desk. "I've just rung there myself."

A chat with Sir Digby Wellow of United Mellemetics had been high on Sloan's list of priorities, and Sir Digby Wellow had left the United Mellemetics factory at Luston for an unknown destination exactly half an hour ago.

◆

12

Constable Crosby plodded across the churchyard at Randall's Bridge. The workmen had gone back to Berebury. They had been exchanged for a posse of uniformed policemen under Sergeant Wharton. They were searching the churchyard for clues. And the inside of the church: but not the tower. The tower, Inspector Sloan had decreed, was to be left severely alone until he came back.

Crosby had dutifully timed the journey from the Osbornes to Randall's Bridge and now he was making for Vespers Cottage and the two Misses Metford.

He hadn't knocked before the door flew open. He followed Miss Mabel inside, brushing against the fronds of a fern in the tiny entrance.

"Mind that," said Miss Ivy sharply.

"It belonged to Mother," said Miss Mabel.

"Forty years we've kept that going," added Miss Ivy.

Crosby shrank to one side—and came up against a bamboo table bearing an aspidistra.

"The sitting room," decreed Miss Mabel quickly.

"This way," said Miss Ivy.

"Last night . . ." said Crosby.

"The poor man in the tower . . ."

"They've just taken him away . . ."

"In a black van."

"We saw him go."

"All covered over."

"We see everything from here."

"Did you see anything last night?" said Crosby, greatly cunning. "Cars, for instance . . ."

Miss Ivy cocked her head to one side. "Not see."

"Hear?"

"We heard one, sister, didn't we?"

Miss Mabel nodded. "We did."

"When?"

"About half-past ten," said Miss Ivy.

"Twenty to eleven," said Miss Mabel.

"It came up by the church gate and stopped there for a bit," said Miss Ivy.

"How long?"

" 'Bout ten minutes," said Miss Mabel.

"Fifteen," said Miss Ivy.

"Did you see anyone?"

Two heads shook as one.

"Too dark," said Miss Ivy.

"Too far away," said Miss Mabel.

"But you heard it," persisted Crosby, looking from one sister to the other. This was worse than Wimbledon.

"We did," they chimed.

" 'Specially when it went," said Miss Ivy.

"It made a funny noise then," said Miss Mabel.

"Funny?" Crosby's head felt like a shuttlecock. He was sitting in a wing chair which had an antimacassar bounded by torchon lace which tickled every time he moved his head. Taking statements wasn't supposed to be like this.

"Louder," said Miss Ivy.

"We don't usually hear cars go," explained Miss Mabel.

"Go?"

"Come," added Miss Ivy. "We hear them come because of the hill up to the church gate."

"It's steep," amplified Miss Mabel.

"When they go . . ." said Miss Ivy.

"Yes?" said Crosby reeling.

"They usually go quietly," said Miss Ivy out of turn.

"Downhill," said Miss Mabel.

"Home," commanded Detective Inspector Sloan as they left the works of Struthers and Tindall at long last.

Detective Constable Crosby slipped the police car into gear and turned out of the gates and into the main traffic stream.

"And slowly," added Sloan, settling himself down in the front passenger seat and opening his notebook.

"Slowly, sir?"

"That's what I said, Crosby. It means," he added trenchantly, "the opposite of fast."

A cone of injured silence encompassed the area of the driving seat. It was practically visible.

"More people," Sloan reminded him presently, "are killed by motorists than by murderers."

"Yes, sir." Crosby slid the car at high speed round a traffic island installed not very long before at the instigation of Inspector Harpe for the sole purpose of slowing down all traffic.

"Besides . . ." Sloan hunched his shoulders forward, "I want to think."

As *amende honorable* went it wasn't exactly memorable but Constable Crosby's obedient "Yessir" came up with just the right inflexion this time.

Not, thought Sloan with foreboding, that the space of one short car ride—however decorous—was going to be anything like long enough to marshal his thoughts ready for Superintendent Leeyes.

There were some things, though, which could be put in hand.

"The firm's van, Crosby. Yesterday lunchtime."

The constable patted his car microphone affectionately. "I've sent a message out. Anyone who saw it to let us know."

"All Calleshire?"

"All cars, sir. After twelve yesterday."

"So Miss Holroyd says," Sloan reminded him. "So she says. We don't know."

That was the police way of thinking.

The way he should be showing this raw constable how to think.

It was ingrained in him now, or so his wife, Margaret, said. In detective work you thought in much the same way as you would pick your way across a swamp, testing for firm ground each time you took a step forward.

He didn't know if what Miss Holroyd—or anyone else in this case, come to that—said was firm ground or not yet.

It was too soon to know, though already things had been said which had sounded a tinkle of warning . . .

He'd have to sort those out, too.

"That all, sir?" Crosby enquired assiduously, steering a perilous course the while between a Calleshire County omnibus and a furniture van.

"The Companies Register," said Sloan when he'd started breathing again. "Then we'll have the background of Struthers and Tindall and Cranswick Processing and all these other people they're doing work for."

"Especially United Mellemetics?"

"Especially United Mellemetics," agreed Sloan, looking at the list. "There's Punnett Tooling, too, and Harbleton Engineering and Marlam's . . ."

"Never heard of them."

"And Stress Engineering."

"Or them."

"What about Leake and Leake?" Sloan frowned. "That seems to ring a bell."

"Vans, sir. They have vans. Lots and lots of them. Little green ones. You see them everywhere." Crosby made them sound like leprechauns.

"Oh, them. I know." Sloan went back to his list. "Osborne is the last one."

"George Osborne," said Crosby. "That'll be his invention. It's going to be a great success. Tindall said so."

"Mrs Osborne said Richard Tindall said so," Sloan reminded him patiently. "How many times do I have to tell you that it's not the same thing?"

Crosby didn't answer. He seemed to be busy turning the police car down Bell Street. They were getting near the police station now.

Sloan was still looking at his notebook. "Now, Crosby," he went on as one encouraging a pupil, "what is the next thing we should do?"

"Eat, sir," responded the pupil with celerity. "It's tummy time."

Sloan snapped his notebook shut. He really didn't know what the Force was coming to.

* * *

Yes, Inspector, a voice agreed down the telephone from the mortuary to the Police Station, they had received the body from the church.

Yes, they had listed the contents of the pockets. They had done that at once because of Dr Dabbe wanting to get on and you know—everyone knew—what Dr Dabbe was like when he was in a hurry . . .

What had there been? Well, the usual.

What was the usual?

Some small change—not much. Keys—house keys by the looks of them.

Not car keys?

Not car keys.

A couple of handkerchiefs. A good boy.

A what?

A good boy. One handkerchief to use and one to spare.

"Anything else?" enquired Sloan in a strangled voice.

Nothing out of the ordinary at all. A wallet, of course. With some money. The business cards in it said Richard Mallory Tindall if that was any help to the Inspector.

It was? Good.

Anything else in the wallet?

A receipt from Adamson's in London.

Not Adamson's the jewellers?

The voice from the mortuary spelled out a famous address in a well-known London street.

Sloan drew in his breath. Adamson's were suppliers to what crowned heads remained in the world, and their lineal successors in the matter of wealth—oil-rich sheikhs, property tycoons, pop stars, pools winners . . .

"What for?" he asked.

Adamson's didn't deal in peanuts, of course. Everyone knew that. Not even in costume jewellery when it came to the point. With Adamson's it would be for real— whatever it was. At Adamson's if it looked like gold, then it would be gold.

A pair of diamond and emerald clips, read out the man at the mortuary, made to order as per pattern supplied.

"What," asked Sloan with mounting eagerness, "was the date on the receipt?"

July 15th.

Tuesday. The day before yesterday.

Anything else?

Well, yes, there was one of those funny little things that looked like a small ruler but wasn't—oh, a slide rule?

Really? Well, there was one of them. And à pen and pencil, and a small diary.

The Inspector would like that sent over to the police station straightaway.

Right.

Will do.

That all? Well, there wasn't anything else.

Nothing?

Nothing. Was there anything else special apart from these clips that the Inspector had in mind?

A box of matches? echoed the voice. From its disbelieving tone matches might have been as rare as emerald and diamond clips. Oh, no, nothing like that.

Not even a lighter.

A man must eat.

Even if he was a policeman.

Pangs of hunger had at last driven Detective Inspector Sloan to agree with this admirable proposition advanced by Constable Crosby, who had assuaged his own appetite minutes ago.

And a detective must detect.

Even if he was hungry.

Sloan was manfully trying to do both at once: cradling the telephone receiver between ear and shoulder, a pen in one hand and a beef sandwich in the other.

"A pair of emerald and diamond clips," he said indistinctly, when his London call came through. "Ordered through your Mr Lee."

Somewhere in a heavily carpeted office in the West End of London Messrs Adamson's, Crown Jewellers, brought their Mr Lee to the telephone.

"A very nice pair of clips, Inspector," Mr Lee began cautiously.

"I should like to know all about them," said Sloan.

He would like to know all about the United Melle-metics file, too. And a lot more about an Italian called Giuseppe Mardoni.

"They were emerald, Inspector. Mr Tindall specified emeralds in his letter. With diamonds if we could manage it." Mr Lee contrived to make the diamonds sound like makeweight.

"Emeralds with diamonds," mused Sloan, taking another bite of beef sandwich while he could.

"Mixed stones are all the fashion again," said Mr Lee. "It's not like it used to be."

"Really, sir?" Sloan wondered if he should have known that.

Was it the sort of thing every good detective knew? There was no limit to those. It was Sherlock Holmes who held that every detective should be familiar with seventy-five varieties of perfume, wasn't it?

Or was it fifty-seven?

Sherlock Holmes had solved his locked room mystery by finding a deadly Indian swamp adder in residence.

Sloan had had no such luck.

So far.

"Emeralds with diamonds," he repeated.

"That's right, Inspector. To match some Victorian emerald and diamond earrings. To pattern, so to speak."

"What sort of clips were they?"

"Let me see now, Inspector—how can I best describe them to you? You haven't got them in front of you, by any chance?"

"No," said Sloan shortly, "I haven't."

"Well, in that case . . ." Mr Lee paused. "They were each composed of cabochon . . ."

"Cabochon?"

"Polished not cut into facets or shaped."

"Right," he mumbled in between beef and bread. "I've got that."

"Cabochon emerald and diamond clusters . . ."

It did sound rather nice, thought Sloan, as he wrote it all down. He tried to visualise a pair of clips like that on his own wife, Margaret. He found it refreshing to call up her image in the middle of the day and was dwelling on this while Mr Lee went on talking.

"I'm sorry, sir," apologetically. "Might I have that again, please?"

"The clusters," repeated Mr Lee with the esoteric enthusiasm of the expert, "were slightly graduated and each was held and intersected by a small diamond collet."

"Collet?" queried Sloan.

"The horizontal base of a diamond when cut as a brilliant," said the expert. "We just had to match the existing earrings, Inspector. Not a difficult job really. We had them to go on. Mr Tindall sent us one and we worked from that and then returned the two clips and the earring."

"When?"

There was a rustle of paper to match Sloan's chewing. "According to our ledger, Inspector, it was dispatched two days ago."

"Tuesday."

"That's right. Mr Tindall mentioned a date in his letter." Adamson's Mr Lee gave a discreet professional cough. "I understand a lady's birthday was involved."

Sloan pushed the description over to Crosby who had just come in. The constable was holding a message sheet which had reached them from Superintendent Leeyes.

"It's about this G. Mardoni, sir." Crosby handled the flimsy paper with care. The police authority economised on the quality of the paper it used and much time and Scotch tape were expended on sticking it together. "It confirms that he was booked on a direct flight to Rome leaving London Airport at one-thirty this morning."

"And he didn't make it . . ."

"Failed to report to either the terminal or the airport, sir." Crosby took another look at the message sheet. "It says here that they're trying to find out if anyone of that name caught a later flight."

"Or G. Mardoni using any other name," said Sloan, picking up the telephone and dialling the Dower House at Cleete.

♦

13

"Me, Inspector?" echoed a Fenella as disbelieving as the mortuary attendant. "The boss of Struthers and Tindall? Oh, surely not. Not now of all times. I couldn't possibly . . . I can't begin to think straight as it is."

Sloan kept the receiver to his ear while she did, perforce, begin to think straight.

"I couldn't possibly . . ." she repeated tremulously.

"I don't know about the Struthers part, miss . . ." It was surprising how skilled you got at interviewing people.

"I remember that my father bought a controlling interest when old Mr Struthers died. His two daughters still have a share, I know, but not a big one."

"What they call a minority interest?" suggested Sloan helpfully.

"That's right, Inspector. They get dividends and things." She still sounded bewildered. "I can't be the boss though, Inspector. Not of the whole firm. It doesn't make sense."

"Did your mother have an interest?"

"Yes, but what's that . . . oh, I see . . . yes. Yes, she did. And she did leave it to me."

"If you inherit your father's holding, too, miss, I can see that you might very well be the majority shareholder."

"Oh, dear . . ."

"Going back to last night, miss . . . When did Mr Mardoni leave you?"

"Just before ten-thirty. He brought me home and then left. He had a plane to catch."

"He had a car?"

"He hired one while he was here. He'd arranged to leave it at the airport. You can do that."

Sloan took down the name of the car hire firm, and asked, "When did he come to England?"

"Last Thursday. He had business in London, he said . . . he's a civil engineer . . ."

He wrote down all the details she gave him. They would have to be checked, of course. Everything would have to be checked. That was what being in the police force meant. Check, check, and check again.

Fenella Tindall, surrogate owner, had been quite willing for Detective Inspector Sloan to have the names of all the firm's clients, Henry Pysden's caution notwithstanding.

"I shall be going back to Randall's Bridge soon, miss," he said obliquely.

"There's no hurry," she responded dully, "is there? Not now."

"I'm afraid not, miss," Sloan agreed tendentiously.

There wasn't either. Not from her point of view. Her father was already dead. All would be still at Cleete. She wasn't beset by furies like Superintendent Leeyes and Dr Dabbe and the police photographers—all of whom were clamouring for his attention at once.

And behind them there would be the baying hounds of the Press . . .

"But I fear that we will want you, miss, to . . . we will have to ask you to look at . . . to say if . . ."

"I understand, Inspector." Her voice was almost harsh, it was so tightly controlled. "I'll be here when you want me."

"It'll be at the mortuary in Berebury."

"I won't run away."

"We're sending a car over for you."

"Thank you."

Sloan cleared his throat. "It's on its way over."

"Now?"

"Dr Dabbe . . . he . . . we can't afford to waste any time, miss. Not in a case like this."

"No . . ." he heard her breath expire in a long despairing sigh. "Of course you can't."

"Miss . . ."

"Yes?"

"There was one other thing."

"Yes, Inspector?"

"Would you mind telling me when your birthday is?"

"In March," she said promptly. "It's March the twenty-ninth."

"Did your father give you a birthday present then?"

"Oh, yes. He wouldn't forget."

"Thank you, miss." He tried another tack. "Do you by any chance own a pair of emerald and diamond earrings?"

"No, Inspector . . ." not quite so promptly.

"Did your mother?"

He heard her catch her breath this time. "Not to my knowledge."

As soon as Sloan had rung off Fenella Tindall dialled the Berebury Grammar School for Boys and asked for Mr Osborne.

"He's not here." A throaty schoolboy voice answered the telephone after a long delay. "It's the dinner hour. There's nobody here."

"Where is he?"

"Out."

"Are you sure?"

"His car's not here," croaked a half-broken voice.

"That doesn't mean a thing," said Fenella bitterly.

"He'll be back by two," offered the boy with all the confidence of the young. "He's got a lesson with us on mass and volume." His voice took a centaur-like leap to manhood. "Do you want to leave a message?"

"Yes, please," said Fenella Tindall.

Superintendent Leeyes was in one of his ivory tower moods.

Sloan knew them of old.

The Chief Constable, who had had an expensive education and who knew the Superintendent very well too,
called them Aristotelian.

All Sloan, who had clawed his way up through primary
and grammar school, knew was that the Superintendent
liked his action offstage. And all over in one day.

Within one revolution of the sun was how it would
have been put by the Chief Constable *pace* Aristotle.

"All going well, Sloan?" enquired Leeyes briskly.

"We've got a general call out for a van and a pair of
diamond and emerald clips."

"Emerald clips?"

Sloan told him about the jewellery.

"Ha! You've got down to the grass roots, then."

Sloan took the point dutifully.

"Murder," enquired the Superintendent, "for a pair of
emerald and diamond clips?"

"There's this missing United Mellemetics file, too, sir."

Leeyes snorted. "Don't say there's something our precious Sir Digby Wellow can't handle."

"Looks like it, sir, and he's disappeared too now."

"What!"

"His firm don't know where he is," amended Sloan.

"So that's this man Cranswick and Wellow who've both
slipped through your fingers . . ." The Superintendent believed in staying on top.

"There are half a dozen firms with hush-hush jobs
farmed out to Struthers and Tindall, and United Mellemetics happens to be one of them, sir."

Superintendent Leeyes looked up suspiciously. "These
people, Sloan—Struthers and Tindall—they're not doing
anything for the War Office, are they?"

Ministry of Defence it might be now. War Office it had
been and War Office it would remain to Superintendent
Leeyes.

"Not that I know of, sir."

"That's something to be thankful for, anyway."

"Yes, sir." Sloan was with him there.

All the way.

Superintendent Leeyes's last brush with Security had
seared its way into the annals of the Berebury Force.

It had been a memorable affair.

The Superintendent had asserted territorial rights with all the vehemence of a mating cock robin and the Security people had—in the end—retreated, muttering into their cloaks and daggers.

"There's this funny business about selling Struthers and Tindall, too, sir. To Cranswick Processing."

"Hrrrrrrmph."

"The girl inherits."

"The King is dead, long live the King," said Leeyes brutally. "Or, in this case, the Crown Princess, I suppose."

"She says she didn't know anything about Cranswick Processing going to buy her father out."

"They all say they don't know anything about anything." Leeyes pointed to the papers on his desk. "No news of the boy friend yet."

"Who, sir?"

"That Itie. Macaroni or whatever he's called."

"Giuseppe Mardoni," sighed Sloan.

That, at least, had been bound to happen.

"Don't like the sound of him, Sloan," said Leeyes equally inevitably.

"No, sir." Sloan hadn't for one moment supposed he would.

Xenophobia, thy name is Leeyes: all the Berebury Police knew that.

And that the Superintendent belonged to the "fog in Channel, continent isolated" school of thought.

If there was a Channel Tunnel where would natives begin then?

"The airport people say they're doing their best at this end," said Leeyes, poking about among the paper in his IN-tray, "and we've been stirring up the Arrivals Department in Rome. Nothing in from them yet either."

"So all we really know," said Sloan fairly, "is that he didn't catch his plane."

The Superintendent had no time for the impartial statement of fact. "Two o'clock was it that those two women saw someone in the churchyard?"

"So they say."

"And we've no witnesses as to the girl being back at the house when she says she was."

"No, sir."

Leeyes leaned back in his chair. "We keep on coming back to the daughter, don't we?"

"The daughter, sir?"

"You heard, Sloan," said the Superintendent testily. "Presumably she stands to gain more than anyone else, doesn't she?"

"I think so, sir," said Sloan, "but at this stage . . ."

"And this expensive jewellery wasn't for her?"

"Apparently not."

"She mightn't have exactly taken to the idea of it being for someone else."

"Even so, sir . . ."

"And then there's this foreign gent."

Sloan had thought that he would crop up again.

"Perhaps," said Leeyes, "her father didn't quite take to the idea of her marrying him. Most fathers wouldn't . . ."

"A touch of the 'O my beloved Daddy's,' you mean, sir?" said Sloan swiftly.

It was Margaret, his wife, who was keen on opera, who bought and played the records. But Sloan listened to them.

"What I mean," pronounced Leeyes largely, "is that seventy percent of all murders are family affairs."

"But not daughters, sir," protested Sloan. "Daughters don't usually . . ."

The Superintendent waved a majestic arm. "There was that one in America, Sloan. Don't forget her. She killed her father. And her stepmother. I forget her name."

"Lizzie Borden," supplied Sloan weakly, though he hadn't meant to.

It was a new idea to Fenella that she might be Struthers and Tindall now.

She stood by the telephone and consciously bent her mind to considering it. She was Struthers and Tindall. Struthers and Tindall. Anything to stop herself thinking about a pair of emerald and diamond clips and a dead father.

The more she thought about it the more she was prepared to agree that it might be so.

Struthers and Tindall.

The policeman—it must have been the quiet one who seemed to be in charge who had been on the telephone—not the young one with the gangling arms—she was quite sorry for him—he seemed to have a penchant for being underfoot without actually doing anything—that other policeman—the first one—could well be right after all. She might indeed be the owner of more shares in Struthers and Tindall than anyone else now.

If she inherited her father's holding, that is.

Emerald and diamond clips.

They obtruded into her thoughts at last—thrusting their way into her unhappy mind like an obstreperous visitor and pushing out all the other thoughts with which she had been trying so hard to fill her mind just to keep them out.

Emerald and diamond clips.

He wasn't even, she told herself, the sort of person who went in for buying jewellery. Even when her mother had been alive. She hadn't known him all her life, so to speak, without knowing that. If, she decided painfully, he had bought emerald and diamond jewellery for someone else he might equally have left the Dower House and his shares of Struthers and Tindall to . . .

She would have to stop thinking, that was all.

She didn't think she could take these sorts of thoughts on top of all the other news of the morning.

She wished she was back in Rome.

Everything was always on such a grand scale there—especially tragedy—that her own small problems would be bound to sink into proportion if she were able to be there. She was sure of that. Put beside the Colosseum and its horrific history surely all the Tindall family troubles would just sink into perspective as little local difficulties.

She sighed.

Fiddling little matters they might seem to be against the backcloth of Roman history but just now they still filled her horizon. What she wanted at this minute was Principessa Trallanti's prescription—a day in the Forum. That was what the Principessa always counselled for anyone overwrought or too beset by the cares of this world.

"A day in the Forum, Miss Tindall, takes the edge off

the present," she would pronounce in her own impeccable English. "I find it never fails to restore what the French call the *sang-froid*. I don't think you have a word for it?"

How very like the Principessa to use one language and then make up for its deficiencies in another—and neither of them her own . . .

Fenella had readily admitted to the shortcomings of English idiom. Actually the young had the phrase the Principessa was looking for. They called it "keeping your cool." She had not told the Principessa this. Though the Trallantis were both more international than any jet set they hadn't quite caught up with the world's youth yet.

The Principessa was quite right.

That was what Fenella wanted.

A day in the Forum . . .

"Miss Tindall, I wonder if . . ."

She'd had one such day in the Forum with Giuseppe Mardoni.

"Call it a Roman holiday," he'd said persuasively.

He was very persuasive.

A long cool spring day under a clear Roman sky with the flowers thrusting themselves out of the interstices of the broken stone; a day spent wandering from one inconsequential colonnade to another. That was the whole point, of course. They were utterly inconsequential those stones now—but once upon a time . . . Ah, once upon a time they had been important—the exact position of each of consequence to somebody.

And today . . . today the stones were just like any ruins anywhere and about as important . . .

"Miss Tindall"—the voice was much more firm this time—"I wonder if I might have a word with you?"

She turned.

Mr Gordon Cranswick was at her elbow. She had no idea how long he had been standing there.

◆

14

The various instruction courses attended by Police Super-intendent Leeyes left their scars in a way which would have astonished the highly skilled instructors who lectured at them had they known.

Like a sticky snail the Superintendent strewed a trail of imperfectly assimilated concepts behind him: not only did they show where he had been but they were a nuisance to the unwary. The latest one which he had gone to—on business management—had proved no exception to this unhappy rule.

Whether the sophisticated ideas of big business—in this case "management by objectives" (objectives: commercial)—could be related to the police force (objectives: law and order) was doubtful. Naturally the course organisers, well able to count potential police heads, did not harp on this point.

As the burden of their spiel lay in measurement they were—from time to time—in difficulties about this. Measurement of commercial success requires only the ability to count. The proof of the police pudding isn't always in the eating. As any Home Secretary knows, measurement of successful police work takes a judicious blend of faith, hope, and charity.

There had been one other aspect of the management course dear to the hearts of the lecturers. It was called

critical path analysis and it had made a deep impression
on Superintendent Leeyes.

He had tried to explain it to Sloan.

"It's a great idea. You work out the right order for
everything before you start doing anything."

Sloan had given it an ear. The Superintendent was
given to instituting new ideas at the police station without much warning, and it was as well to be prepared.

"Then," enthused Leeyes, "you don't waste time going
over the same ground twice."

Sloan had been temperate in his response. Nothing was
ever as easy as that.

"All you have to do," the enthusiast had amplified, "is
to decide what's got to be done and then work out the
best order to do it in."

Sloan put the telephone down now after talking to
Fenella Tindall and tried to do just that.

It wasn't easy.

What might pass for good organisation in a biscuit
factory might not be the best course of action in a murder
hunt.

There was a pair of emerald and diamond clips unaccounted for—a pair of emerald and diamond clips
which, after all, hadn't been a birthday present for
Fenella Tindall. And if the receipt in his pocket was anything to go by, last seen with Richard Mallory Tindall.

There was a secret report about United Mellemetics
about which much the same could be said. Unaccounted
for and last seen with Richard Mallory Tindall.

There was an unknown Italian gentleman—and you
couldn't, thought Sloan wryly, have a more sinister phrase
than that. He and his wife, Margaret, were conscientious
visitors of museums and art galleries. "An unknown
Italian gentleman" sounded like the title of a Renaissance
painting. Anyway, whoever he was he had been careless
enough to miss his aeroplane last night—the night on
which Richard Tindall died. Sloan wasn't sure yet whether
he ought to be worried about Giuseppe Mardoni or not.

There was—or rather, there wasn't—Gordon Cranswick, notable for his anxiety to buy Struthers and Tindall
as speedily as possible—an anxiety which seemed to have
dated only from yesterday afternoon. Mr Gordon Crans-

wick would have to—Sloan dredged up another oft-repeated phrase from the Superintendent's Management Course—Mr Cranswick would clearly have to be gone into in depth.

Sir Digby Wellow was another in some sort of unavailable limbo. No one at his firm knew where he was and the Luston police couldn't find him either. Sloan wanted to talk to Sir Digby Wellow pretty badly.

There was Paul Blake, the handsome young man who hadn't done yesterday's work to order. He was the one, Mrs Turvey had said, with an eye to the main chance. Not, Sloan reminded himself acidly, that that should be thought a purely criminal characteristic . . .

There was a man called George Osborne, missing now and not at work yesterday lunchtime either . . .

And there was Fenella Tindall who knew who it was the emerald and diamond clips were for—or he, Sloan, Calleshire born and bred—was a Dutchman.

And over in the village of Constance Parva there was someone who was nothing at all to do with the late Richard Mallory Tindall who was dipping a pen in pure vitriol to the consternation of all and sundry, but especially the sensitive.

The Mayor—Sloan unconsciously straightened his shoulders—at least he knew where the Mayor and his little troubles came in any critical path analysis of explaining Richard Tindall's sudden demise.

Then there was Richard Tindall himself, done to death all alone in a church tower, his solitary end engineered at dead of night . . .

Sloan paused in his appreciation of the situation.

Engineered.

Now he came to think of it it would take someone like an engineer to arrange for the Fitton Bequest to be poised so finely that it would fall on Richard Tindall at a given time and place—like when he was lying where he had been—at a moment when there was no one there to push it over.

He noted the thought and then put his plan of campaign into action.

* * *

Fenella started.

"If I might just have a word with you, Miss Tindall."

"I have to go to the mortuary, Mr Cranswick." At least he was less peremptory now.

"Oh, I see . . ." He paused, and then waved his hand. "I'm very sorry about—er—all this."

She braced herself.

That was another thing she would have to endure.

Sympathy.

She wasn't at all sure that she could take sympathy on top of everything else that had happened.

Something Shakespearean came unbidden to her mind. Something appropriate, of course. He was always appropriate. That had been his genius. What was the line?

"Of comfort, no man speak."

She found to her surprise that she must have said it aloud.

Gordon Cranswick sounded surprised, too.

"Er—quite. Quite. I apologise. I am bound to be an intruder at a time like this . . ." He sounded expectant but Fenella said nothing so he hurried on: "In the ordinary way, you realise, I should not have bothered you. You must be wondering why . . ."

Fenella inclined her head in what she hoped was a gesture of polite interest.

"It's your father's firm, Miss Tindall . . ."

"Yes?"

"I think you should know that yesterday afternoon he said that he would sell it to me after all."

"After all?"

He cleared his throat portentously. "Cranswick Processing have been interested in Struthers and Tindall for some time. We had been putting out feelers and so forth . . ."

He made it sound, thought Fenella rather wildly, like an Italian marriage.

"It was a natural move at this stage in our development," said Gordon Cranswick, oblivious of her train of thought.

(Just like an Italian marriage, decided Fenella.)

"My Board were right behind me, of course."

(Parents and all.)

"We took advice in the financial aspects, naturally."

(They did that in Italian marriages, too. First. Naturally.)

"And the long-term prospects looked sound."

(They didn't begin negotiations in Italy unless they were happy about the future.)

"We had—on our side anyway—already gone into the ramifications of any—er—union."

(In-laws.)

"And our solicitors were prepared at any time to meet with Struthers and Tindall . . ."

(The honest broker?)

"It seems," continued Cranswick weightily, "as if the outcome would be to our mutual advantage."

Fenella nodded.

People always said mutual when they meant that they themselves benefited and didn't mind too much whether you did or not.

"Mind you," added the businessman, striking a cautious note, "Cranswick Processing have some prior commitments which would have to be taken into consideration."

(In an Italian marriage contract it would be Great Uncle Mauro's doctor's fees.)

"As I am sure Struthers and Tindall have, too."

(And, in the other family, Cousin Luigi who wasn't quite right in the head.)

"Of course"—Gordon Cranswick cocked his head inquiringly—"we may not be the only people in the field?"

(It was customary in Italy to establish first whether there were any other suitors.)

"That makes a difference, of course."

(It made a difference in Italy, too.)

She became aware that Gordon Cranswick was looking at her this time as if he expected a positive response.

"Er—I'm sorry." She started. "I was thinking about something else. You were saying that a marriage had been arranged . . ."

Gordon Cranswick stared at her. "I was talking about a takeover, Miss Tindall. Of Struthers and Tindall."

"So you were. I'm sorry." She pulled herself together. "My father hadn't said anything to me, Mr Cranswick, about selling Struthers and Tindall to anyone."

Yesterday she might have had the emotional energy to have felt hurt and angry about this.

But yesterday was a long, long way from today—farther than she would have thought possible—farther than the distance from the Palazzo Trallanti in Rome to the Dower House in Cleete. Her mind could take in that difference in space easily enough. Today—the today that was so far from yesterday in time—today she found she had no more feeling to spare.

"He always said no to me," responded the businessman frankly, "until yesterday afternoon. Then he changed his mind and said he'd sign on the dotted line today. Must have been almost the last thing he did before . . . before . . ."

"Not quite," said Fenella astringently, a pair of emerald and diamond clips thrusting their way back into her mind.

"Oh? Anyway, that's why I'm here. And now," he went on, not urgently, "I need to know with whom to deal. You do see that, Miss Tindall, don't you?"

Fenella's hand strayed back towards her white bead necklace. How had that quotation gone on? There was a passage after those words about no comfort which she remembered having to learn too.

Long ago, it was, in another existence, when she hadn't a care in the world. In a chalky schoolroom, it had been, from a woman teacher who—she now realised—probably wasn't as desiccated as she seemed—when the whole class had been as detached from life and as cosseted as young queen bees in a hive.

Their Shakespeare class had been for something irrelevant called General Education.

There was a sudden crunching of car tyres on the gravel drive. Fenella looked out of the window and saw Police Constable Hepple going out to greet another policeman. There was a policewoman sitting beside the driver.

Perhaps, thought Fenella, appreciating Shakespeare—the real man—marked a stage in everyone's development. By the time he was relevant you were no longer young and innocent.

That play—about no comfort—had been *King Richard II*. It was all coming back to her now. She could hear the voice of the English mistress as the words tumbled back into her mind and the rest of the quotation came to her: "Let's choose executors and talk of wills."

That was the moment when Police Constable Hepple came in to announce that the car had come to take her to the mortuary—and found Gordon Cranswick there.

And when Gordon Cranswick insisted with something of a return to his old manner, "I want to buy the company, Miss Tindall. Now. And I'm not going to take no for an answer. Your father said I could and that's good enough for me."

"But, Mr Cranswick," she said, "how do I know that?"

The search—police-fashion—of the premises of Struthers and Tindall at Berebury's Wellgate was being conducted by the portly middle-aged Police Sergeant Wharton. His team had moved from the churchyard at Randall's Bridge.

It was no different from other searches anywhere else.

Sergeant Wharton ended up staring dispassionately at the crop of incongruities reaped during it.

It was a strange harvest and some of it was not his concern.

Like the reading matter of one of the technicians in the Testing Department who was apparently cherishing body-building notions. Wharton looked the man up and down and decided he wouldn't do for the Force, not unless his subscription had a good bit to go . . .

Or the small bar of plain chocolate kept by Miss Holroyd in a drawer quite clearly marked *Carbon Paper*.

Or the crossword puzzle—nearly completed—on the desk of someone else.

Some of it was his concern.

Like the books which the firm's accountant was standing over like a stag at bay. Wharton had sequestrated them nevertheless—without being unduly impressed. In his experience accountants were given to defending with their lives figures which could be seen by anyone in the published balance sheet; and it would take another accountant to establish whether there was anything to hide or this behaviour pattern was just habit.

The photocopy was his concern.

It was of one of Struthers and Tindall's patents and it had been folded neatly inside a telephone directory in Paul Blake's room. Sergeant Wharton gave his man full marks for finding that.

And Paul Blake none at all for his vehement denials that he knew anything about it.

Overdone, Wharton thought.

The experiment on which Henry Pysden was working was his concern. On sea-water magnesia, or so he was told. Wharton followed his instructions and noted the model number and the name of the makers of the time punch machine attached to the apparatus.

There was the petty cash which the office boy had put into his own pocket. But this, he insisted, he had only done as a precaution because there were so many policemen about.

"None of that, young man," Wharton had said with dignity, "or I'll take a magnifying glass to that old scooter outside. It is yours, I take it?"

The youth had paled into silence and Wharton had continued his stately way.

The foreman of Testing was speechless at the interruption to work but vocal about the police, the heat, United Mellemetics . . .

Wharton had pinned him down about United Mellemetics.

He—the foreman—didn't know what all the fuss was about. He had set up some experiments on detailed instructions from Mr Tindall last week. They were to do with the strength of pipes, their tensility, testing to see how ductile they would be under certain specified conditions—that sort of thing. The tests had been duly done and the results sent back to Mr Tindall.

The next thing he knew about them was this morning when Mr Pysden was round saying someone had lost the ruddy file. That was just before they heard the sad news about Mr Tindall. Well, he, the foreman, had certainly given the United Mellemetics stuff back to poor Mr

Tindall; not that he could very well confirm it now, could he?

When.

Yesterday morning. The foreman didn't hesitate. The Wednesday. Put all the workings and results on Mr Tindall's own desk, he had, himself, and if anyone was going round saying anything different he would like to be told this minute . . .

Wharton, primed by Sloan, asked at what stage Paul Blake had checked the calculations.

The foreman assumed an expression which would have been recognised the world over as that of any seasoned noncommissioned officer on being given the opportunity to comment on the efficiency or otherwise of a junior officer. He very nearly took it, then discretion raised its careful head.

"Mr Paul Blake," he said precisely, "came down to Testing on Monday and checked our calculations, and also some which Mr Tindall had done himself."

Sergeant Wharton looked at the foreman man-to-man. "Everything all right there I take it?"

"Or I'd want to know the reason why," said the foreman comfortably.

Sergeant Wharton went back to Henry Pysden's room.

One thing was apparent from the search.

United Mellemetics might not have existed at all for all the physical traces it had left at Struthers and Tindall.

He took out his notebook and said to Henry Pysden: "I'll begin with you, sir, if I may. I need to know exactly where you were between the hours of ten-thirty last night and two o'clock this morning . . ."

◆

15

Fenella Tindall wasn't worried about her tummy. At least, not in the way Detective Constable Crosby had been.

In her case lunchtime had come and gone unremarked by either hunger or food. If she felt anything at all it was slightly sick.

That would be the smell of antiseptic in the mortuary.

She had already forgotten everything about the journey from the Dower House at Cleete to the police mortuary at Berebury. She had travelled there in silence beside an experienced policewoman who knew better than to try to distract her with kind words.

And she had walked into the mortuary in such an aura of disbelief that it was as if she were standing outside herself as she did so—watching dispassionately as a slight girl with auburn hair wearing a brown dress and a necklace of white beads took the few steps between car and door. It might have been someone else—not Fenella Tindall at all—she felt so detached.

The mortuary attendant said: "This way, miss," in totally matter-of-fact tones.

Fenella followed.

As she did so a tall good-looking young man uncoiled himself from beside the doorway.

The policewoman watched impassively as he went to Fenella's side.

"Paul!" Fenella halted. "How kind of you to come."

Paul Blake made an awkward gesture with one hand and with the other propelled her gently along the passage after the mortuary attendant.

"Sorry about all this," he said. "Thought I'd better turn up."

The white-coated figure of the mortuary attendant disappeared down the passage and through another door beyond that. The smell of antiseptic got suddenly stronger, welling up ahead of them as they followed him.

"Oh . . ." Fenella gave way to a momentary pang of surprise as she saw the white-sheeted figure in the mortuary.

Paul Blake moved up behind Fenella and murmured, "It won't take a minute."

"Now, miss . . ." the man lowered his voice, "if you'll just take a look . . ."

He needn't have bothered to speak in undertones. Fenella wasn't listening anyway. She was thinking about something else.

About Italy.

She'd seen death there, but it had been different. Not clinical and antiseptic like this. Not with clean white coats wrongly speaking of life not death. In Italy death was dark and medieval. The men near it—the Misericordia—were garbed in long black robes and hooded save their eyes. It was a dress which went back to the Plague.

She took a look at the face revealed by the mortuary attendant and nodded.

"That's my father."

She would have liked to have said it was her grandfather whom she had seen—death had added a generation to her father's face.

"Richard Mallory Tindall," she said in as firm a voice as she could manage.

"We can go back now," said Paul Blake.

Actually the face Fenella wished she didn't have to look at was the mortuary attendant's.

She now knew why it was those men of the Misericordia—the Brethren of Mercy—were covered all over in black except for their eyes. It meant that the bereaved saw no face round the deceased—no face to associate forever with moments like these. It would have meant that she would have been spared the memory of the mortuary attendant chirpily steering them back to his little office.

"Just one more thing, miss, and then we're done. Little matter of his effects."

She stirred involuntarily at the word and then remembered.

The dead didn't have possessions, they had effects.

She became aware that he was asking her to identify some objects laid out in an orderly row on a table. There was some small change, his house keys, a wallet, a few notes, a slide rule, a pen and pencil, two handkerchiefs . . .

"Sign here, miss, please, that they're his."

She made a slight movement away from the proffered form. "They're not all there. There was his diary. It's a little leather one. I gave it to him. He always carried it with him. Always . . ."

The mortuary attendant sucked his teeth. "That's gone to the Inspector, miss. He wanted that double quick."

Detective Constable Crosby handed the diary—duly fingerprinted—to Detective Inspector Sloan.

Sloan took the small leather covered book and turned to Wednesday, July 16th.

That was yesterday.

Was it only yesterday?

His eye strayed involuntarily to Saturday, July 19th. That was the date engraved on his mind.

Show Day.

He looked out of the Police Station window and sighed. This strong sunshine would be bringing his Princess Grace of Monaco along too soon. She was a perfect rose, of course, but if it stayed as hot as this for too long she was going to be a perfect rose on Friday not Saturday.

"If you look under Wednesday, sir . . ." Crosby was getting restive.

Sloan switched his gaze back to the left-hand page. There was just one entry in the little oblong space with that date on it. It was quite brief.

It said: *G. 12.30.*

"That's going to be a great help, Crosby, that is.
G . . ." he said ruminatively. "G for Giuseppe, do you
suppose?"

The Superintendent, he was sure, was going nap for
Fenella.

"Or G for Gordon?" countered Crosby brightly.
"That's that fellow Cranswick's name, isn't it?"

"Or G for Osborne?" said Sloan.

"G for Osborne, sir?"

"George Osborne. He who has a wife and an invention."

"Oh," Crosby subsided. "I'd forgotten about him."

"A good police officer," Sloan reminded him, "can't
afford to forget anything."

"No, sir."

"Ever."

"Yes, sir."

Sloan put the diary down and moved over to the wall. A
large-scale map of Calleshire hung there.

Crosby joined him. "We know, sir," he said eagerly,
"that he left his works at twelve."

"Miss Holroyd said he did," murmured Sloan, un-
heeded, "which isn't quite the same thing."

"That gives him half an hour," continued Crosby, missing the point.

"Fifteen miles at the outside," said Sloan.

"Twenty, sir. Surely."

"In an old van," Sloan reminded him. "Not in a
souped-up police car with you at the wheel."

"Fifteen then," conceded Crosby.

"So where does that get us?"

It didn't get them very far.

Mahomet had agreed to go to the mountain.

Police Constable Hepple had been very persuasive. Not
for nothing had he mastered the art of the quiet life. And
the first rule for a quiet life is to arrange for all action
to take place somewhere else.

Anywhere else.

That was how it was that Mr Gordon Cranswick found

himself being interviewed by Detective Inspector Sloan at Berebury Police Station. In this case "being interviewed" was something of a euphemism. It seemed at times as if the boot might be on the other foot.

Mr Gordon Cranswick, Chairman and Managing Director of Cranswick (Processing) Limited, was not only firmly planted in one of Sloan's office chairs, but was also making it quite clear that he wasn't going to budge from there until he himself took the decision to do so. He was, in fact, very busy demonstrating the fact that when Mr Gordon Cranswick was around Mr Gordon Cranswick took the decisions, sundry police detective inspectors notwithstanding.

"Now, what is all this about?" he demanded as soon as he set eyes on Sloan.

"The death of Richard Tindall," said Sloan mildly.

He asked Cranswick what had brought him to Cleete.

"What brought me? Tindall, of course. Well, Struthers and Tindall, I suppose, to be strictly accurate."

"The firm rather than the man?"

"It's the firm I'm interested in. Literally. Have been for some time. Just what Cranswick needed—their sort of business would back up our sort of business very nicely."

"Your sort of business being . . ." enquired Sloan.

"Processing." He waved a hand. "Oh, I know that processing covers a multitude of sins but in the case of Cranswick it means that we take a patent belonging to a customer and do the lot with it."

Sloan was guarded. "The lot?"

"Develop, manufacture and market. Struthers and Tindall are primarily testers."

"So they would go rather well with you."

Cranswick nodded vigorously. "We realised that when we added up what we were paying them for their feasibility studies and so forth."

"So?"

"So I set about trying to buy them." Cranswick sat back in his chair. "I won't say it was easy."

"Oh?"

"Tindall wasn't all that keen on selling at first and then his wife died and that changed things a bit."

Sloan nodded. It would.

"And then," the businessman stirred irritably, "something else cropped up."

"Tell me."

"Another buyer."

"Who?"

"Tindall wouldn't say. Just told me that he'd had another offer better than mine."

"You believed him?"

Cranswick shrugged. "Why not? I could always prove it by leaving him with it if I wanted to."

"You didn't want to?"

"I did not. I wanted Struthers and Tindall and I knew I'd have to pay for it. It's a good firm, you know. Sound. But it wasn't going for a song."

"So someone else wanted it, too."

"Pretty badly, I should say, from what they were willing to offer. Still, I reckoned that if it was worth it to them it was worth it to me."

"Quite," said Sloan. People wrote books on political economy but in the end decisions came down to homespun yardsticks like this whatever the professors had to say. "So in the end yours was the better offer?"

"No," said Gordon Cranswick unexpectedly, "it wasn't. They—whoever they were—were prepared to overbid me."

"But . . ."

"But," he said heavily, "Tindall wasn't prepared to sell to them. Said he'd found out something about their methods which he didn't like and if my offer was still good he'd take it."

"When?"

"Tuesday evening."

"Where?"

"Ah," Gordon Cranswick leaned forward. "That's just it. He rang me from a call box and suggested a quiet meeting somewhere simple where nobody knew us."

"At twelve-thirty yesterday?"

"That's right. At Dick's Dive. It's a transport cafe halfway down the Calleford road—on the way to Luston . . ."

"We know it," said Sloan. All policemen knew all transport cafes in their area.

"Actually," admitted Cranswick, sounding surprised, "the food was pretty good."

"It has to be," said Sloan, "or the customers vote with their wheels."

"What? Oh, yes, of course . . . Well, that's where Richard Tindall told me that he was willing to cut these other people out and sell to me at my last offer and on my terms . . ."

"On your terms?"

"I wasn't prepared to be hamstrung by any silly agreements about keeping people on. I run Cranswick my way and if the Struthers and Tindall people didn't like it they would have to go . . ."

"These other people who wanted to buy, he didn't tell you who they were or what methods he didn't like?"

Cranswick's brow wrinkled. "Not exactly but he did say I needn't worry. He'd deal with them before he left."

"And then?"

"Then I went back to Town to see my bankers and solicitors and arranged to come down here first thing this morning to sign on the dotted line."

Sloan nodded and pushed his notebook into a slightly more prominent position. "Now, sir, if you would tell me exactly where you were between ten-thirty last night and two o'clock this morning . . ."

The next call Sloan had was from the mortuary.

Dr Dabbe was ready for him.

Being Dr Dabbe it was a case of being ready and waiting.

"I've started on some of the groundwork, Sloan. That blood on the floor, for instance, was Tindall's all right. And it had splashed down while he was lying there. While he was alive, of course. There was no more blood after the sculpture came down. That was what killed him."

Sloan nodded.

"I should say he was hit a yard or two short of the

sculpture—say just inside the door—and then dragged across the floor until he was lying practically beside the sculpture. As to what he was hit with . . ."

"Yes?"

"You couldn't call the edges of the wound well-defined but whatever it was it was enough to knock him out—sorry—render him unconscious—got to mind my p's and q's with you people . . ."

Sloan grinned. There was English, Police English and medical words, and nobody knew this better than the pathologist.

". . . Say something like an old sock filled with sand—I'll look out for grains of sand presently. And the blow was well aimed."

"Just the one?"

The pathologist nodded. "And from behind."

"A weapon," remarked Sloan, "would be nice."

"Nothing to touch 'em with juries," agreed the doctor. "Now, Sloan, I think you'll be interested in some mental arithmetic I've been doing. Algebra, really."

"Oh, yes, Doctor?" Sloan was wary in his response this time. Police work was one thing. Algebra was quite another.

"You can do any equation if you know all the quantities, of course."

"Yes, Doctor." He agreed to that readily enough.

"You can do quite a few with one unknown quantity."

"I'm sure you can, Doctor."

"And you can do one or two with two or more unknowns."

"Can you, Doctor?"

"Our equation, Sloan," said the pathologist, waving a hand at the sheaf of papers which Burns, his assistant, was working on, "concerns the time of death of Richard Mallory Tindall."

"Good."

"Our known factors are what the deceased had to eat at seven-thirty last evening . . ."

Sloan nodded. That wasn't exactly blinding him with mathematics.

". . . Confirmed by Mrs Marcia Osborne, plus a drink, the time he had it and the size of the drink." Dr Dabbe raised his eyebrows appreciatively. "Talk about dishy. Our Mrs Osborne's quite a stunner, isn't she?"

"I couldn't say, Doctor," said Sloan a trifle stiffly. "I sent my Constable."

"Bad luck. Still, you'll have to go again, I daresay. Her old man still hadn't shown up all through the dinner hour, did you know that?"

"I did."

"Sorry. I forgot it was the close season for suspects. Your bird, of course. Where was I?"

"Doing an equation."

"Oh, yes. Food plus time lapsed after its consumption equated to state of digestion of deceased gives you the time of death." Dr Dabbe twiddled a pencil. "And if that's not good enough there's the state of the brain tissue. That's always good enough."

"Always?"

"Given these factors," said the pathologist, ignoring this, "all I had to do then was to work on his stomach and brain and one or two other oddments and put them down, too, and bob's your uncle."

"Your equation?"

"Exactly. Narrows the time of death very nicely."

Sloan turned back the pages of his notebook to his record of his interview with the two spinsters at Vespers Cottage by the churchyard.

"Would I be very far out, Doctor, if I said it was somewhere about two o'clock this morning?"

"You would," said Dr Dabbe placidly. "Very."

"Very?"

"Two and a half hours out. Give me those papers, Burns."

Sloan stared at him. "Two and a half hours? That means you make it . . ."

"According to my equation," said the pathologist, still amiable, "which Burns here has just finished checking and which I am prepared to read out in open court, I make the time of death pretty near eleven-thirty last night."

"How near?" enquired Sloan.

"As near as dammit," said the pathologist graphically.

◆

16

There was quite a plaintive note in Detective Constable Crosby's voice.

"What I don't understand, sir, is why this guy who did it . . ."

"Yes?" It was funny, reflected Sloan, how the very word "murderer" stuck in your throat . . .

How you didn't use it unless you had to . . .

Not even Crosby . . .

Not even now they'd done away with the death penalty . . . and they'd got the life penalty instead.

Well, the quarter life penalty. It wasn't really life any longer . . .

Sloan made himself stop thinking about prison sentences.

It upset him too much.

They'd stopped talking about them at the Police Station long ago.

"What about him, Crosby?"

"Why didn't he just hit him a bit harder the first time and be done with it?"

"I don't know."

"So what this guy did then, sir, was to arrange for this great lump of stuff to fall while Tindall was lying dead to the world in the right place underneath it?"

"That's all, Crosby."

Perhaps there was something to be said for a certain simplicity of approach, after all . . .

"So," said Crosby, negotiating a right-hand turn, "it's just a case of how and who, sir, then, is it?"

"Don't strain yourself, will you?"

"Oh, and why, sir?" added the Constable seriously.

"Strictly speaking," amended Sloan fairly, his sarcasm evaporating as quickly as it had conjured itself up, "I suppose we don't really need to know why . . ."

"Don't we?"

"But," he added sardonically, "the jury like it."

Sloan thought back to the bloodless crumpled figure lying on the church tower floor and wondered how much motive they were going to need to make head or tail of that.

He dismissed the image immediately.

Between them he could be sure that the cynics and the psychiatrists could explain everything.

He was a policeman and he should know that by now.

The constable was talking again.

"It'll tell us who, sir, won't it, if we can find out why?"

"I hope so, Crosby," he replied heavily. "I'm sure I hope so."

There was always that. Perhaps the boy was learning something after all. Sloan scratched his chin and glanced down at his notes.

There was no help there.

They were as meagre as a Spanish anchor.

"At this rate," he added pessimistically, "we'll just have to ask whoever did it to tip us the wink on how he did it when we've got him."

"Yes, sir."

"Because—quite apart from why—I'm hanged if I know how you arrange for a sculpture to be pushed over without being in there to do it."

"The little window," suggested Crosby helpfully.

"The little window," agreed Sloan. "We've got as far as that already. Somebody put that ladder up against the wall and poked something through the window and knocked the Fitton Bequest off its plinth and then drove the deceased's car back to Cleete."

"But not the night fisherman at two o'clock this morning."

"At approximately ten minutes to eleven," said Sloan crisply, "someone was there doing something and they were gone by eleven if the evidence of the schoolmaster and those two dotty women is to be believed and he died at approximately eleven-thirty . . ."

They would have to take Dr Dabbe for Gospel—however inconvenient—because everyone else would.

". . . when Gordon Cranswick was having a nightcap in his room in his hotel in London, Paul Blake tucked up in bed at his lodgings, Mrs Osborne tucked up in bed with Mr Osborne, which isn't evidence, and Henry Pysden kipped down at the works after doing his bit on his experiment . . ."

". . . and Sir Digby Wellow, Giuseppe Mardoni and Fenella Tindall unaccounted for," finished Crosby.

Sloan looked at him with disfavour. Crosby was getting more like the Superintendent every day.

"There are one or two interesting events in Richard Tindall's last forty-eight hours, Crosby, which have not, I hope, entirely escaped your attention . . ."

"Losing that file at the works," he said promptly. "The United Mellemetics one."

"The purchase," said Sloan, "of a pair of emerald and diamond clips . . ."

"And," Crosby chipped in, "him deciding to sell the business to Cranswick Processing."

"Plus the discovery that someone was trying to buy the firm by methods he didn't like. Someone else."

"That and getting himself done," added Crosby simply.

Sloan abandoned his train of thought. "We mustn't forget that, must we?"

The next two reports to come in were both about the Italian, Giuseppe Mardoni.

One was from London.

The Metropolitan Police had checked as requested with the car hire firm from which Mardoni had rented the car he had used in England. They reported that the vehicle had been returned as arranged to the airport. The time of the check-in had been just before three o'clock in the morning.

The second came from Inspector Harpe and asked Sloan to drop by when he was near the Traffic Department.

"I may be wasting your time, Sloan," began that worthy with characteristic pessimism, "but I thought you might like to know that two of my patrol boys turned something up about Wednesday night."

"I would."

"They were chatting up the blokes at the all-night garage on the Calleford road . . . they always keep in well with them . . ."

So much, thought Sloan, for all those voluntary advisers of the police who thought traffic should be separated from police work.

They forgot that man was now a motorised animal.

"The garage had a call-out to a foreign gent late last night."

"Did they?" responded Sloan alertly. "And what time was this, may I ask? Did they remember?"

" 'Course they remembered," said an aggrieved Harpe. "Just about half-eleven. Very excited, they said the chap was. All over a puncture."

"He had a plane to catch," remarked Sloan absently. "Did you say puncture?"

"A flat, anyway. The garage didn't repair it. They just changed the wheel for him. Put the spare on and got him going again."

Sloan flipped back through his notes. "Couldn't he change a wheel? I thought he was an engineer of sorts—oh, no. A civil engineer."

"Couldn't see to change a wheel," said Harpe. "No torch."

Sloan sighed. "And where was all this?"

Inspector Harpe rolled his eyes expressively. "Need you ask, Sloan? It was where they laid the tar on the Berebury to Randall's Bridge road in the morning. It's always like this when the County have had a go at the road. Punctures and windscreens shattering for days afterwards. Nothing but trouble."

Sloan nodded briefly. Happy Harry wasn't the only one with troubles. There was nothing easier to contrive than a flat tyre. Someone in Mets was going to have to go round to the car hire firm at the airport and check if that puncture had been genuine or a convenient alibi.

"Half-past eleven," he said, "and Fenella Tindall says he left her at half-past ten at Cleete. I wonder where the hour went."

"I can tell you that," rejoined Harpe. "Walking along the Berebury road in the dark looking for a telephone kiosk. He'd be a good three miles from anywhere there, wouldn't he?"

"Couldn't he have got a lift?"

"That road isn't exactly Piccadilly Circus after dark now, is it, Sloan? Anyway, who's going to pick up a foreigner at that hour of the night? For all we know he may look like Sweeney Todd."

"Machiavelli, more like." Sloan sighed. Neither of them knew what he really looked like, though there was nothing he himself would like more this minute than a sight of Giuseppe Mardoni. "And then he'd have to find out who to ring."

"There was some sort of handbook in the car with addresses and so forth."

"So he could read and speak English all right . . ."

"Looks like it."

"I thought he might." Sloan made another note in his book.

Perhaps Giuseppe Mardoni had become a little less nebulous now but he was still shadowy.

Everyone in the case seemed just out of reach.

Giuseppe Mardoni.

George Osborne.

Sir Digby Wellow.

At least Gordon Cranswick was more substantial now than he had been. Heaven only knew where he'd got to, now, though. Luston, probably, thought Sloan morosely, to make an offer for United Mellemetics. They couldn't keep him at the station, for all that the Superintendent would like to have done. And Cranswick would know that . . .

"Perhaps the airport people will come up with something," he said to Happy Harry. "There's always a chance of that."

But there was no comfort to be had from that Jeremiah.

"Makes it difficult, doesn't it?" agreed Harpe with a melancholy nod. "How are you getting on with the Tindall end of things?"

"All I want there," said Sloan with feeling, "is some idea of how you arrange to kill a man without being there to do it. Half an hour after you've gone away, in fact."

"He wasn't starved to death, was he?" enquired the Traffic Inspector with interest. "I read a book once about a millionaire who died shut up in a gymnasium with plenty of food. Starved to death. Proper mystery it was, too. What these Indians had done was to hoist his bed forty feet up in the air with pulleys and then let it down again after he'd died . . ."

The Superintendent's reaction to the news about Giuseppe Mardoni was immediate, predictable and not without glee.

"Complicity, Sloan. I've said so all along."

"Er—who with, sir?"

"The girl, of course. She drives the car back to Cleete. He waits behind in the churchyard and pokes something through the little window and then sets off for the airport."

"And the two o'clock trip? There was someone about then, sir."

"A fisherman. Like those two old women said."

Sloan didn't tell Superintendent Leeyes that he'd already sent Crosby off to see the angling people. Both lots—the Calleshire Freshwater Club and the River Calle Angling Society—to see if they had any night fishing competitions laid on. Or if they knew if any of their members went fishing at two o'clock in the morning on Thursday.

Nothing would surprise him about fishermen.

Nothing.

And he didn't want any case of his to founder on the life cycle of the roach.

When he came to think about it being aware of the close season for coarse fish wasn't all that far from Sherlock Holmes and his seventy-five varieties of perfume.

"What about the other alibis?" asked Leeyes.

"Henry Pysden's is the only one that's cast iron. The others are a bit—er—circumstantial, sir. Even Sir Digby Wellow's . . ."

That had been something of a delicate chat.

And it wasn't what he'd joined the Force for.

Ringing a titled lady he'd never seen to ask if she'd spent the night with her husband, while Crosby set about discovering the private life of the trout.

Lady Wellow's voice had been cool. "I heard the odd snore, Inspector. Through the wall."

"Er—yes, of course, madam—er—milady."

"We have separate rooms. My husband likes a hard mattress—for his back, you know. I like a soft one."

Sloan had tapped his pencil to an old metre.

> *Jack Sprat could eat no fat,*
> *His wife could eat no lean,*

Why were there nursery rhymes everywhere he looked today?

Not that there was anything particularly childish about Lady Wellow's tone.

It was ironic, detached.

"Are you trying to tell me, Inspector," she had said, "that Sir Digby spent the night somewhere else?"

"No, milady."

> *And so betwixt them both, you see*
> *They licked the platter clean.*

"Only trying to be sure that he spent it in Luston."

"I see. He grunted when he took his shoes off. He always does. I heard that, too."

"When?"

"About midnight."

That wasn't evidence, either, of course.

Not yet, anyway.

It would be soon.

If the reformers got their way.

When a husband could give evidence against his wife and vice versa.

When you wouldn't be able to tell the Criminal Court from the Matrimonial one.

He didn't know if that was a blow for Women's Lib or not.

The Superintendent had started up again. He had a piece of paper in his hand.

"The handwriting people say those letters from Constance Parva are all written by the same person."

"So far," said Sloan. "They won't stay that way for long."

There was nothing more infectious than a poison pen. Once the idea cottoned on all manner of people would be taking to it. Old scores would be settled by the dozen. Pale—and not so pale—imitations would hurtle round the village before long, seeding as fast as Enchanter's Nightshade.

"And that shoe, Sloan . . ."

"The golf course one?"

"They've found its mate."

"Where?"

"Behind the fourth green."

"But nothing else?"

"Not yet," said Leeyes ominously.

The next two messages were both for Detective Inspector Sloan.

Both concerned the transport cafe on the outskirts of Berebury near the junction of the Luston and Calleford roads. It was called simply Dick's and all the heavy transport in the western half of the county used it. Its bumpy potholed car park was the only place for miles around where there was room and to spare for a dozen lorries and their trailers.

The first was in the form of a report from one of Inspector Harpe's traffic patrol car drivers. He had noted a small grey van parked at Dick's yesterday. The van answered to the description of the radio message issued at thirteen hundred hours. He had observed it at the

Transport Cafe at about dinnertime yesterday. At about half-past twelve.

The second message wasn't couched in anything like so stately terms.

It had come from Dick himself.

In a hoarse, hurried voice.

"A bloke," he said, "in a car on the park. Dead. Thought he'd had a heart attack, they did. Until they saw the hole in the back of his head."

DIAMONDS ARE OF MOST VALUE
THEY SAY THAT HAVE PASSED THROUGH
MOST JEWELLERS' HANDS.

◆

17

Even as he crossed the car park of Dick's Transport Cafe,
Sloan appreciated what a choice spot for murder it made.

Giant articulated trailers obligingly screened the car
in which the dead man lay from the view of all but those
who passed very near. It was parked well away at the
back, beyond two Continental trailers resting on their way
to Rumania.

It had been the Rumanian drivers who had spotted the
crumpled driver and—to their eternal credit—who had
then drawn attention to him.

"Take their numbers," ordered Sloan automatically,
"and everyone else's. Nobody to leave the place until I
say."

He had help this time.

Two of Inspector Harpe's men, whose patrol car was
never far from this stretch of main road, were there for
the asking. They would take all the numbers and stop
anyone slipping away from the cafe. At the moment it
looked as if—rather than go—everyone at Dick's had
decided to stay.

They were all clustered round a large black car.

"We get all sorts here," said Dick, the proprietor. He
was referring to the opulence of the car and its gleaming

chromium. "Nowhere else to eat and park for miles."

"Had he been in?" asked Sloan.

The cafe owner shook his head. "Not that I'd noticed."

The dead man was slumped forward over the steering wheel, folds of flesh overlapping a tight collar, his face an unhealthy white. Sloan went round and peered in through the windscreen. Even his best friends might not have recognised the man now—not with his glazed eyes staring sightlessly at nothing and his jaw hanging slackly downwards.

Sloan certainly didn't.

The car had a Calleshire registration number, though.

"Crosby, take this number and find out who the car belongs to."

He turned to the watching crowd of men.

"Anyone see anything?"

Nobody answered. One or two at the edge of the crowd started to drift back towards the cafe.

"Anyone notice how long this car has been here?"

This was more productive.

A driver and his mate with strong Yorkshire accents hadn't seen it when they had hauled their giant load onto the forecourt.

" 'Bout 'alf an hour ago that would have been, mate. At least. Happen a bit more. That's us over there." He pointed to a loaded lorry. "Hobblethwaite Castings. T'car wasn't 'ere then."

The time of their arrival was confirmed by Dick himself.

"Two pies and peas, wasn't it, lads?"

They nodded.

"Just finished them, we 'ad, when we 'eard there was summat up out 'ere."

"You won't get quicker service on the road anywhere in Calleshire," said the cafe proprietor proudly. "Nobody waits long for his dinner at Dick's."

Sloan cut this commercial short. "Anyone notice any other private car on the park?"

Nobody had.

Crosby came back from sending his radio message about the car number and Sloan packed his audience back into the cafe with Inspector Harpe's two men.

Then he turned to Crosby. "Well?"

"Hit hard on the back of the head, sir." Crosby peered forward. "No weapon in sight."

"We'll search for that presently. Anything else?"

Crosby took another look. "Was he hit here, sir? In the car?"

"Looks like it." Sloan stared at the big car that had everything: including room to swing a cat. Or a weapon.

"You could do it from the back seat easy, sir. Plenty of elbow room."

"Anything else?"

"Not very long ago?" offered the Constable tentatively. "The engine's still a bit warm."

"It isn't the only thing," said Sloan. The sun was getting hotter by the hour.

"Nothing else to see," reported Crosby.

"Pity," said Sloan. He hoped that the Superintendent's famous exchange principle would still hold good.

"And no signs of a struggle."

"Someone he knew perhaps . . ."

Both policemen were still standing looking at the dead man when the police radio in their car started to chatter.

"Foxtrot Delta one six, Foxtrot Delta one six . . ."

Crosby went over to the car and made an answer.

The voice of the girl at the microphone in the control room at the Constabulary Headquarters in Calleford echoed nasally across the cafe forecourt.

"Foxtrot Delta one six . . . the car number which was the subject of your enquiry of fourteen thirty-seven hours . . ."

Sloan listened impatiently. Time and number, that was all County Headquarters cared about. That and making a record of everything.

The girl's voice droned on, oblivious of his thoughts ". . . is registered in the name of the firm of United Melle-metics Limited, Jubilee Works, Luston, Calleshire . . ."

Fenella wondered how it was that she could ever have thought that the Dower House had seemed empty before. It was nothing then to how it felt now.

The same police car which had taken her to the mortuary brought her back to Cleete. It was inevitable, she supposed, that their route had lain through Randall's Bridge. All roads to the south crossed the river there. There was no other way. Even so she could have wished that they did not have to pass that grey square tower . . .

Why the church at Randall's Bridge anyway . . .

She shook her head ever so slightly. She knew the answer to that. Someone had told her. The Detective Inspector. She remembered now. It was when she was still thinking in terms of an accident.

Not an accident, he'd said, hadn't he?

When she'd asked why it was that the sculpture hadn't just slipped.

Ever so kindly he had explained that heavy sculptures don't just slip on their own at eleven-thirty at night in church towers that may or may not have been locked—and that they slip more easily still if they happen to have had little wedges driven under their plinths to help them on their way . . .

The house echoed to her footsteps as she walked through it again. Her first thought was to open a few windows. Even an hour with them closed on a day like this gave the building a stuffy shut-up feeling. The policewoman had offered to stay with her but Fenella had declined. Mrs Turvey, too, had gone home. She had a husband to feed, but she would be back. Fenella knew that.

The house seemed so empty that presently Fenella began to find the feeling oppressive. She took herself out into the garden. Gardens never felt quite so empty in the way that houses did . . . there weren't objects everywhere you looked which reminded you of people who weren't there any more.

She wandered about looking for somewhere to sit. There was too much sunshine for any of the usual places. Besides, living in Italy had conditioned her to seek shade not sunshine.

She gave a short laugh to herself.

Who would have thought that so brief a time in Italy would have made such an impression on her?

She would go back.

Not straightaway.

When everything here at Cleete had been sorted out.

When the police had got to the bottom of all that had happened.

When they had found out the naked truth.

Once she'd wondered why people called the truth naked but not after she'd been north to Florence from Rome with Principessa Trallanti and the children.

The Principessa had watched her enjoy Florence, take in the mellowed red roofs, the black and white churches, the sculpture and the paintings before remarking in her dry, precise English: "Everyone, Miss Tindall, is either a Florentinian or a Roman at heart. One or the other. Never both. Even Signor Mardoni."

The last had been because of Giuseppe Mardoni. Roman to his fingertips, his frequent visits to the Palazzo Trallanti had been noticed even by the Principessa.

Much as Fenella herself loved Rome she had plumped for being a Florentinian.

"Most English people do," the Principessa had said, unsurprised.

It was on that visit to Florence that she had seen the Naked Truth.

In a picture in the Uffizi Gallery.

A Botticelli.

The picture wasn't called *Truth*. It was called *Calumny*.

It was a painting of a mythical Hall of Justice, with an enthroned judge. Only this judge was seated between two figures representing Suspicion and Ignorance. Two other figures—Spite and Calumny—were dragging a naked figure—Truth—before the judge. Duplicity and Deceit were attempting to adorn Truth, while a grim figure—old and dressed in deep black—called Penitence—looked on.

"They're all women," she remembered stammering to the Principessa.

But that worldly noblewoman had seen nothing out of the ordinary in that.

Nor in Penitence's mourning garb.

"But she's so . . . haggard," insisted Fenella.

"You are still young, Miss Tindall." The Principessa had raised a hand that was gloved in spite of the heat. "In time you will see what penitence does to people."

Fenella found a nice patch of shade under an old beech tree and settled herself there. She could see the front of the house from where she sat and it was as good a place as any to be while she considered what had to be done. Her father had some cousins still—they would have to be told—so would her aunts—her mother's sisters . . .

She heard a car crunch up the drive and from her position under the trees saw a man get out and go up to the front door. He seemed to ring the bell and then step back quickly and do something with his hands in front of him.

She stayed where she was.

When there was no answer to his second ring he stepped off the gravel drive and onto the grass and repeated the action.

Fenella froze into immobility.

What he was doing was taking photographs . . .

The Press.

He must be from the Press.

A reporter.

She watched as he made his way round the house taking pictures as he pleased. He didn't catch sight of her shrinking against the bole of the beech tree though, and eventually he went back to his car and drove off.

It must have been something over half an hour after that when another car drew up at the Dower House. She did stir herself then and walked over towards it. She'd recognized the woman who'd got out of the car. Only one woman of her acquaintance would have set out for the depths of the country in the middle of the afternoon in a heat wave so impossibly overdressed.

Marcia Osborne.

Fenella made her way across the grass as Marcia picked her steps carefully over the gravel towards the door bell. Fenella almost grinned. The gravel wasn't so rough but no doubt Marcia's shoes weren't up to anything stronger than carpet. They never were.

"Fenella! Cooooooeeeee . . ."

Marcia had seen her at last and turned away from the front door and the painful gravel towards the grass.

Now that she was nearer Fenella could take in the full splendour of her outfit. Marcia Osborne was wearing a grey silk suit shot with green which was very very smart. Her handbag and gloves and shoes tied up with the green colour in the suit in a way that must have taken days of careful matching. The whole ensemble was topped by a wide-brimmed hat designed to make absolutely sure that not a single ray of sunshine beat down on Marcia's precious complexion.

It was the wide-brimmed hat which concealed the earrings from Fenella's view at first. Fenella herself would not have considered wearing earrings at teatime but she was not particularly surprised that Marcia had them on. Marcia was like that. And her earrings, inherited from her Great-Aunt Edith, had frequent airings.

She had nearly reached Fenella—having done the lawn very little good with the heels of her shoes on the way—before Fenella got a really good look at her.

What she saw sent a cold shiver down her spine.

Besides the earrings Marcia was wearing a pair of matching clips.

They were unmistakably emerald and diamond.

◆

18

"Who?" howled Superintendent Leeyes. He was never a man to count up to ten anyway.

"Sir Digby Wellow," repeated Sloan.

He was tired of saying the name now. He'd said it again and again and had been met on all sides with shocked disbelief. There was a posse of incredulous men even now on their way from Luston making all possible speed just to confirm this very fact.

Not that Sloan himself was in any doubt. Not since he'd heard who the car at Dick's Cafe belonged to, and done a few calculations. Sir Digby Wellow must have left Luston just before Sloan had tried to telephone him there.

"Wellow of United Mellemetics?" asked Leeyes. He had come back to the news after his weekly session with the Chairman of the Watch Committee. "The one whose secret file is missing from Struthers and Tindall?"

"That's the one," said Sloan, adding flatly, "and he's been murdered too."

"This file then . . ." began the Superintendent excitedly.

"Is still missing." Sloan finished the sentence for him. "Struthers and Tindall have turned their place upside down and still say they can't find it. I had the whole building properly searched and Sergeant Wharton can't find it either."

"But what was in it, man? That's what counts." Spar-

161

ring with the Watch Committee Chairman always made Leeyes tetchy. What it did to the Chairman Sloan could only imagine.

"Your guess, sir," responded Sloan evenly, "is as good as mine. Or anyone else's, sir, come to that. As I said before all the paperwork—even the scrap—is kept with the file and goes back to the customer. And Struthers and Tindall keep no records. That's even part of their contract apparently."

"Someone must have worked on it, Sloan."

"Paul Blake and Richard Tindall himself."

"Well . . ."

"Blake says that all he did was to check some workings that Tindall had done on the coefficients of expansion."

"United Mellemetics must know," said Leeyes.

"No, they don't," countered Sloan, who had had a long telephone conversation with a bewildered deputy chairman at United Mellemetics. Edward Foster had sounded to Sloan like one of those who have had greatness thrust upon them . . . unless he had got the way he had through perpetually working in the shadow of the forceful Sir Digby Wellow.

"But . . ."

"United Mellemetics didn't even know Sir Digby had taken one of their problems to Struthers and Tindall, sir. Could have been anything, this chap Foster said."

"He must know what sort of work they've got on the go there, Sloan." Superintendent Leeyes always knew what was going on in his manor.

Sloan consulted his notebook. "Foster says they've just designed a new instrument for checking the performance of a solar energy source to provide impressed current for cathodic protection of underground pipe lines."

"Nice work," said Leeyes cordially, "if you can get it."

"And another," pursued Sloan, "for measuring internal corrosion rates of lines."

The Superintendent took a deep breath and rapidly reduced the situation to police level. "Sir Digby Wellow sends an unknown problem to Struthers and Tindall and Richard Tindall goes and gets himself murdered in this peculiar fashion."

Sloan agreed.

"Then the file on this unknown problem disappears."

"Yes, sir." That was true, too.

"Then," declared Leeyes incontrovertibly, "Sir Digby Wellow gets murdered as well."

"Yes, sir."

There was no denying that, either. Dr Dabbe had been and gone and said the same thing about the body on Dick's Cafe forecourt.

And muttered about the wound. The pathologist wasn't prepared to commit himself at this stage but the two head wounds had a lot in common.

"Someone arranged a meeting there," went on Leeyes. "Set up the whole thing, I daresay."

"I think so," said Sloan carefully. "It's where Tindall met Gordon Cranswick yesterday, too."

"After which," remarked Leeyes with celerity, "he came back to Berebury having told this fellow Cranswick he was willing to sell out Struthers and Tindall to Cranswick Processing?"

"So Cranswick says, sir. So Cranswick says."

This time when he got back to his own room again there was only one piece of paper on Sloan's desk.

It was the slightly tattered critical path analysis which he had drawn up that morning after the finding of Richard Tindall's body in the church at Randall's Bridge.

He looked at it for a long moment and then laid it gently on one side.

Critical path analyses took no account of suddenly dead Chairmen in Company cars on the forecourts of good pull-ups for carmen.

Then he had a second thought.

It could go the same way as the normal distribution curves which had so intrigued Superintendent Leeyes the month before. He punted it across the desk and into his wastepaper basket, sent for Crosby and a car, and got down to business.

"Luston first, Crosby. United Mellemetics' Jubilee Works. And then back to Struthers and Tindall. Any more news from Dick's Cafe?"

"They're still taking statements out there, sir."

"Get some photographs for them, too. Show them one of everybody."

"Everybody?"

"The lot," repeated Sloan wearily. "The Mayor, too, if you like. Paul Blake, Gordon Cranswick, Henry Pysden, this fellow Osborne, that Italian . . . Interpol will get you a photograph of him—and Sir Digby, of course."

"Sir Digby, sir? All the people at Dick's Cafe have seen him already."

"He didn't look like he did today yesterday," Sloan reminded him grimly. "His own mother mightn't have known him today."

"No, sir."

Nor Lady Wellow, thought Sloan, making a note.

Sir Digby wouldn't be grunting when he undid his shoelaces tonight. Somebody would have to talk to her, too, soon.

Crosby swung the police car out onto the big roundabout on the outskirts on Berebury and pulled over towards the Luston road.

There was one other matter on Sloan's mind.

"You put someone to keep an eye on those two odd old women at Vespers Cottage, Crosby, didn't you?"

"Yes, sir. Like you said. An unobtrusive watch."

"I think they're material witnesses," said Sloan. "Not that I particularly want them in court for Defence Counsel to play with."

"No, sir." Crosby changed gear.

"And someone who could kill Richard Tindall and Sir Digby Wellow would kill them without batting an eyelid. In cold blood." Sloan scratched his chin, recalling something. He went to lectures, too. Not as often as the Superintendent but now and again. In the line of duty. At one of them he'd heard the lecturer say something about how a man killed . . .

"But, sir," Crosby interrupted his train of thought, "what they saw was at two o'clock this morning. Dr Dabbe says Richard Tindall was killed at half-past eleven last night."

"Dr Dabbe," said Sloan tersely, "only has to report on his findings. You and I, Crosby, have also to do a little thing called solve the case—which is something quite different."

"Yes, sir."

Blinkov had been the name that the lecturer had quoted. Sloan had remembered it because half the audience had thought the speaker had been having them on. Blinkov the Russian. Cousin to Inoff the Red, a billiards man had suggested derisively.

Blinkov, if he remembered rightly, had argued that the coarse murdered coarsely, the refined and delicate temperament found a way of doing the job in a refined and delicate way.

And the scientific scientifically?

Sloan glanced down at his notebook.

"Do you realize, Crosby, that all these men we've been dealing with have something in common?"

"No, sir."

Sloan sighed. At least Crosby never pretended to knowledge that he hadn't got. Perhaps in an odd sort of way that was something to be thankful for.

"They're all clever types, Constable, that's what." His mind went back to the church tower. "Very clever types you might say."

Crosby assented to this. "That was a clever way to kill someone over at Randall's Bridge, sir. Getting that sculpture to fall on the poor chap without being in there with him to do it at the same time."

"You can say that again." Sloan ran his finger down the list and wondered what Blinkov would have made of it. "Henry Pysden and Paul Blake are working scientists. We know that. And George Osborne's the Physics Master at the Grammar School. Who's gone round to keep an eye on him when he does turn up, by the way?"

"Appleton, sir."

"Good." Sloan went back to his list. "Gordon Cranswick and Sir Digby Wellow presumably know their technical stuff seeing that they're heads of scientific firms."

He paused.

Logic demanded that he strike the late Digby Wellow off any lists he was making now. But his scientific knowledge might still be a factor.

He shrugged his shoulders.

It was all very well for Dr Dabbe to give him all that guff about factors and equations. In this case he still didn't know what was a factor and what wasn't. And you couldn't do equations without any factors at all.

"Then there's the . . ."

Crosby saw a woman making for a pedestrian crossing and raced her to it.

Sloan closed his eyes. "Then there's the Italian," he said again. One day some one would write to the Home Secretary about the way this particular police car was driven. "Even he's an engineer of sorts."

"Roads," said Crosby, "that's what they're good at, isn't it, sir?"

"A civil engineer. That's what the girl said he was."

"That's roads, isn't it, sir?" said Crosby.

"It is," agreed Sloan wearily. As a sounding board, Detective Constable W. Crosby definitely lacked something.

"That," said Crosby insouciantly, "just leaves the Mayor then, sir, doesn't it?"

Sloan folded up his notebook. "I suppose it does, Crosby. I suppose it does . . ."

"He's a gents' outfitter . . ."

Fenella Tindall gave Marcia Osborne afternoon tea.

They carried it out under the beech tree because Fenella found the house stifling and everything at which she looked there redolent of her father. It was scarcely cooler in the garden at this time of the day but under the beech tree's shade it seemed so.

"You're to tell me to go away," insisted Marcia from time to time, "if you'd rather be alone."

"Of course not," Fenella replied wanly.

Marcia meant to stay.

Anyone could see that with half an eye.

"And say if there's anything you want doing."

Fenella thanked her with due gravity.

That was easier than explaining that there was nothing she wanted except peace and quiet and a chance to mourn her father decently and in private. And to mourn without worrying about emeralds and diamonds, or the destiny of a small family firm which had somehow tumbled overnight into her lap.

"Sugar?" Life being what it was Fenella poured out tea instead.

Tea was something that she hadn't learnt to do without in Italy. Countless small cups of black coffee throughout the day were no substitute for tea.

"I daren't, my dear. I just daren't." Marcia Osborne patted her wasplike waistline. "Too, too fattening."

Fenella kept a mechanical smile on her face. That, too, she found, was easier than changing her response to whatever Marcia said next. A veil—a black veil—was what she could have done with just now. Then she could have just nodded or shaken her head as the spirit moved her. That would have kept Marcia Osborne happy . . .

"And he was so alive and well last night," Marcia was saying wonderingly. "He was just as pleased about George's patent having come through as if it had been his own. They were as excited as two little boys."

Fenella nodded at that. Her father had been a whole man—generous-spirited and ready to share in other people's joys and sorrows . . .

She saw that Marcia's lower lip was trembling. "We're all going to miss him a lot, Fenella. Poor Richard."

Amen to that, seconded Fenella silently.

But the centre of Marcia Osborne's small universe was still Marcia Osborne and inexorably all events were seen in that particular perspective.

"It would have to happen today of all days and spoil everything . . ." she said.

"Today?" enquired Fenella bleakly.

Marcia Osborne gave up the struggle to stop her lower lip from quivering and said tearfully. "It's my birthday."

She started to fumble about in her handbag and at the same moment the telephone bell back in the Dower House started to shrill.

"I've got a spare handkerchief . . ." offered Fenella, getting to her feet to go indoors to answer the telephone.

"No, it's not that." Marcia fished something out of her bag. "It's this."

Fenella stared. She was looking at a small presentation

box bearing the name of Adamson. Marcia pointed to the matching pair of emerald and diamond clips.

"They were such a lovely surprise," said Marcia in a choked voice. "It would all have been quite perfect except for . . . for the other thing."

"A lovely surprise," echoed Fenella tonelessly.

"They match my earrings perfectly. They—George and your father—took one of them, you know, without my knowing—I never even thought—to send to Adamson's for a pattern. I quite thought I'd lost one of Great-Aunt Edith's earrings and I was really upset . . ."

The telephone was still ringing in the distance.

Marcia sniffed audibly. "I was going to show them to you today anyway. They're my birthday present from George. Your father did all the arranging for him on the strength of the patent coming through and so that it should be a big surprise. Aren't they lovely? Fenella . . . what on earth's the matter? Fenella, stop laughing like that this minute . . ."

◆

19

In due course the police car with Detective Constable Crosby at the wheel trickled through the outskirts of the industrial town of Luston. The pattern of traffic had changed from tractors to articulated trailers and heavy lorries but Crosby forged on. They found the firm of United Mellemetics' Jubilee Works in a part of the town even more industrial than the rest.

There was no doubt at all about whose Jubilee the works were named after. However modern their production methods, the United Mellemetics building was pure Sixty Glorious Years. And it wasn't only the architectural design—Victorian Imperial Neo-Gothic—which dated it. The philosophy of Her Late Majesty's reign was also well to the fore. Only in the days of the Old Queen would the sentiment—couched in bad Latin—*Labore et Profitas*—have been so conspicuously carved in stone over the arched entrance.

Sloan found a good deal of un-Victorian hand-wringing going on in the management offices.

"In fact, sir," he reported back to the Superintendent on the telephone, "the whole firm's running around like a chicken that's had its head chopped off."

Leeyes grunted.

"I don't think," continued Sloan, "that it ever occurred to anyone here that Sir Digby would die."

169

"One of the Immortals, eh?"

"Well, they did call him God. Or so I'm told. Behind his back, of course."

"Did they, indeed? Well, which of them didn't like him enough to kill him? Tell me that . . ."

But Sloan hadn't been able to answer that question. From what he could make out Sir Digby Wellow had been one of those larger-than-life characters who hadn't inspired dislike so much as sheer exhaustion.

"They don't want to buy Struthers and Tindall, too, do they?" enquired the Superintendent.

"They haven't said."

"They've got a couple of rivals if they do."

"A couple?"

"Your friend Gordon Cranswick isn't the only one after the firm."

"Oh?" said Sloan alertly.

"Some outfit by the name of Hallworthy's want to buy it as well. They've just rung the Tindall girl from Birmingham to say so. Made her an offer. Told her they'd been after it for quite a while. And she rang us."

"Birmingham?"

Leeyes was irate. "Sloan, do you have to repeat everything I say."

"I was thinking, sir," he said hastily, "that Birmingham is a long way from Berebury."

"I know it is."

"Too far for these people—what did you say they were called?"

"Hallworthy's. The Hallworthy Small Motor Company, Birmingham."

"Too far for them to have heard about Richard Tindall in the ordinary way." Sloan looked at his watch. "We missed the one o'clock news and the evening papers would scarcely have got hold of any of this yet, even if they're on the streets by now which I very much doubt."

"Well?"

"Someone went out of their way to tell them specially."

"Ha," said Leeyes, "a nigger in the woodpile?"

"More likely just a spy in the camp," said Sloan moderately, "but interesting. Very interesting. Tindall told Cranswick that he didn't like the other people's methods.

They could be the other people and a spy in the camp could be what Tindall didn't like. And that was why he was offering it to Cranswick Processing."

"And what," enquired Leeyes heavily, "have Cranswick Processing and Hallworthy's Small Motors got to do with United Mellemetics?"

"I don't know."

Leeyes grunted. "Well, on past performance if I were Chairman of either company I wouldn't walk under any ladders for a bit. Who's in charge at United Mellemetics now?"

"The Deputy Chairman's a man called Edward Foster, though I wouldn't say," added Sloan doubtfully, "that he's actually in charge . . ."

The unfortunate Edward Foster struck him as being like a man making a gallant attempt to steer a rudderless ship.

"The Board," Foster kept on saying to Sloan, "the Board. I've called a Board Meeting. To decide what to do now. We need a Board Meeting . . ."

Sloan was less sanguine. He didn't suppose the Board would know what to do without Sir Digby any more than the works did.

"If my constable might just start to go through Sir Digby's papers, sir, in case there is any reference at all to Struthers and Tindall there which might give us a lead . . ." Crosby could keep a weather eye open for any mention of Cranswick Processing and Hallworthy's Small Motors, too, but Sloan didn't say anything about that to Edward Foster.

"By all means. Go ahead." Foster ran a hand distractedly through his hair. "We've already had a quick look ourselves without finding anything. I'm not surprised— and it doesn't prove anything either way. Sir Digby never put pen to paper if he could help it. You couldn't say he was one for paperwork at all . . ."

Tycoons, in Sloan's experience, rarely were.

"Or for confiding in people," added Sir Digby's deputy painfully.

"So," said Sloan to Crosby as he showed him Sir Digby's office, "there's not a lot of hope of your finding anything useful here either. Seems as if the big boss played his cards close to his chest all the time. I can't say," he added, "that I blame him. Foster doesn't strike me as man to exactly lean on . . ."

That was one thing that didn't happen in the Police Force. You didn't have anyone undermining your authority.

Not after the moment when you first stepped into uniform.

You were on your own, all right, then, whether you liked it or not.

You and your notebook and the Name of the Law.

Crosby was still thinking about Edward Foster, Deputy Chairman.

"Probably never had a chance, sir. Not with a chap like Sir Digby Wellow breathing down his neck all the time. I'd rather have had Tindall myself from the sound of things."

"Pysden seemed able to handle things quite well," agreed Sloan. He pushed open the door of Sir Digby's room. It was pretty plush.

Crosby, too, took a look round the late Chairman's office.

"Well, there's one thing I must say, sir. It's better to be a big bug in your own rug than a little bug in someone else's rug."

"Quite the philosopher, aren't we?" said Sloan tartly.

There was much work—police work—to be done at United Mellemetics but Sloan proposed to leave that to someone else. There were detectives in plenty attached to Luston Division. They could take statements, note who had been doing what and where at the material times and tell him when they came up with something.

If they did.

Crosby hadn't found any mention of Struthers and Tindall anywhere in Sir Digby Wellow's room.

"Or of Cranswick Processing or Hallworthy's Small Motors either, sir." The Detective Constable climbed into the driving seat of the police car and switched on the radio in one automatic movement. "I don't know where we go from here . . ."

"Struthers and Tindall. That's where it all started . . ." He paused as a message started to come up on the radio and then relaxed again.

"The White Swan, Calleford," announced the girl at Headquarters laconically. "Trouble . . ."

Somewhere in Calleford Division a car would peel off its route and go and sort out the trouble at The White Swan.

"They aren't the only ones with trouble," remarked Crosby, tapping the radio receiver affectionately. "What about us, Doris, dear? Trouble? We've got two murders, a take-over battle, and dirty work at United Mellemetics for a start . . ."

"Their file is missing," said Sloan. "That's all. We don't know what was in it yet."

"But it stands to reason, sir . . ."

"No, it doesn't, Crosby. Not to reason." If there was a word he didn't like to hear used lightly that was it. "Not yet."

"Sir?"

"All we actually know about the United Mellemetics file so far is what we have been told about it and that is not evidence . . ."

The radio had started chattering again.

"Three nines call," said the announcer. "Injury at the bottom of Kinnisport Hill. C.A.B. attending . . ."

That would be the Calleshire Ambulance Brigade having its customary race with the police boys to see who could get to the scene first.

"There is one thing we have got though," said Sloan martially. "One thing we've always got."

"What's that, sir?"

"The old adage that crimes are usually committed by those who benefit from them."

Crosby's brow furrowed. "The daughter?"

"Among others . . ."

"Bravo Delta One Three," interrupted the radio appositely. "Bravo Delta One Three to go to Fourteen Hart Crescent, Luston. A domestic."

". . . she won't be the only one who benefits. There'll be others. Bound to be."

"The Italian?" offered Crosby promptly.

Sloan sighed. He had been right about Crosby and the Superintendent. They thought alike.

"Perhaps. Perhaps not," he said. "There were big changes about and change doesn't always suit everybody." He waved an arm. "It works both ways. There are always those who gain and those who lose by it."

"So," said the constable, "we're back where we started, aren't we?"

"Except," remarked Sloan acidly, "that instead of one dead man we've now got two." It was difficult to know if Crosby was trying to be helpful or not. "And not everyone will call that progress . . ."

The newspapers would have a field day tomorrow: especially if the reporters had caught Superintendent Leeyes in a combative mood, warmed up for the fray by a couple of rounds with the Chairman of the Watch Committee.

"But," said Crosby thoughtfully, "if Dr Dabbe is as right as he thinks he is . . ."

Counsel for the Prosecution and Counsel for the Defence would fight that out in open court—and they would phrase the sentiment better: but not much.

". . . then, sir, we've only got one bloke with a cast-iron alibi, haven't we?"

"Henry Pysden," supplied Sloan, "who was working his time machine at Berebury when the doctor thinks Richard Tindall died. Sergeant Wharton is checking on the time machine alibi."

"Which leaves us rather a lot of people without one," concluded Crosby.

The radio suddenly came to life again.

"A member of the public," said Doris, the announcer, "having it out with Traffic Warden Number Five in Berebury High Street."

"Someone will do that man one day," forecast Sloan, "and I only hope that I don't have to take them in for it."

"Near the traffic lights," directed Doris.

"If it's nobody else's job," remarked Crosby gloomily, "then it's a policeman's . . ."

"He's a bit stroppy," Doris informed the radio circuit informally.

Sloan was bracing. "We're Society's maids-of-all-work, Crosby, and you might as well get used to the idea. There's another thing it's like . . ."

"Sir?"

"Women's work. It's never done . . ."

"Number Five isn't very happy either," added Doris, confident that Number Five would have switched off while he dealt with a turbulent member of the public.

"Now," said Sloan, "Hallworthy's Small Motors of Birmingham. What we need to know is their link with Struthers and Tindall . . ."

Sloan and Crosby were so engrossed in the possibilities of this that they didn't hear County Headquarters the first time they called them up.

"Foxtrot Delta One Six, Foxtrot Delta One Six," repeated Doris patiently. "Have you got Detective Inspector Sloan on board? Come in, Foxtrot Delta One Six. Constable Hepple would like to talk to you at Randall's Bridge. He thinks you should see the Captain of the Tower."

The wizened figure standing in the nave just outside the tower in the church at Randall's Bridge didn't look like the captain of anything to Sloan. He had a bent back and a leathery face and he was called Nathan Styles.

"Caught me at me dinner, 'e did," he said, pointing an accusing finger at Police Constable Hepple.

"Did he now?" said Sloan. "Well?"

" 'Appen I had a bit of a look round for 'im like Earnie 'ere said."

"And what did you find?" So the worthy Hepple was called Earnest, was he?

"Nothing much amiss in 'ere."

Sloan nodded. "That's what Mr Knight told us this morning."

Nathan Styles dismissed the Church Secretary with a jerk of his shoulder. "He's not a ringer."

"The bells?" said Sloan. "Is there something wrong with the bells?"

Nathan Styles shook a grizzled head. "No, it's not that."

"Well?"

"There's an extra rope."

"What!"

"One too many."

"Where?"

"Hanging down the middle." Styles stepped forward into the church tower. It was tidier now than it had been earlier.

Sloan followed him and stared up the shaft of the tall tower.

Nathan Styles pointed aloft with a gnarled and none-too-clean finger. "Up there. The thin one."

Sloan could see the one he meant.

Hanging down was a very thin length of something. It wasn't rope. From where he stood it looked as if it could be twine.

Say fishing line.

It was black and practically invisible. Sloan took a second look at Nathan Styles. He must be pretty sharp eyed.

And know his bell tower.

"If you doesn't believe me," rasped the old man, "you can always ask Charlie Horton. He'll tell you the same. T'wasn't there when we rung Sunday."

"I don't suppose it was," agreed Sloan softly. "I don't suppose for one moment that it was. Or that you've had your practice night this week yet?"

"Not this week," agreed Styles. "Friday's practice night."

"It's a tidy length."

"Seventy feet," said the old man promptly. "Buy the ropes by the foot we has to do so I knows. Cost a lot do ropes, I can tell you."

Sloan peered up into the dimness. "It's too far and too dark up there to see how it's fixed . . ."

Nathan Styles jerked his shoulder upwards. "Daresay it's hitched round one of the bell beams."

"We'll have to get up top and have a proper look." Sloan turned to Crosby and Hepple. "It looks as if it comes straight down all right."

"Shall I go up the tower, sir," offered Hepple, "and see what I can see from up there?"

"Not yet." Sloan waved a hand. "Later. There's a little

experiment I want you both to do first. You, Hepple, go outside and find that ladder, and then get up to that little window from the path side. And you, Crosby, go and get hold of something that we can use to get the end of that twine over towards the window."

Hepple crunched away. Crosby moved off down the church and reappeared a few moments later with a church-warden's stave.

"Will this do, sir?"

Sloan sighed. Justice being, in his view, only a very short head behind godliness and rather ahead of cleanliness, he supposed it would have to.

He took the stave and held it up to the twine. With the flat head of the stave he showed Crosby how to steer it towards the little window above the outer tower door. As he did so the familiar face of Police Constable Hepple appeared at the window.

Crosby continued to walk in Hepple's direction.

Hepple thrust his hand through the embrasure and caught the twine.

"It just reaches the window, sir," reported Crosby over his shoulder. "Exactly."

"I thought it might," said Detective Inspector Sloan.

◆

20

It was Sergeant Wharton who rung the makers of the time punch machine being used by Henry Pysden in his experiment.

They were faintly affronted at his enquiry.

"But we guarantee that the mechanism is accurate, Sergeant. That's what it's there for. It's one of those tied to both a time clock and a personal signature."

"Why?" enquired Wharton.

"Evidence that the readings from the experiment were taken at the right time and by the right person."

"Does that matter?"

The man cleared his throat. "In some types of very accurate experiment it reduces some of the room for error if one person and one person only takes all the readings. It keeps the personal interpretation element down to one, doesn't it?"

Sergeant Wharton supposed it did.

"Very important in this case," said the voice. "Or so we were told when we were asked to set it up."

"Were you?" said Wharton, interested.

"Struthers and Tindall checked with us first—and that it was proof against tampering."

Wharton coughed. "And it is?"

"One hundred percent," responded the manufacturer's

man unhesitatingly. "It's got twin seals with a built-in bonus highly popular with policemen."

"I'll buy it," said Sergeant Wharton.

"We apply the seals and give the guarantee, and we can tell if anyone's been playing about with them—even if anyone else can't."

"Belt and braces," observed Wharton who was so weighty that he didn't need either.

"Buttons, too, if you like, Sergeant. We don't leave anything to chance here . . ."

Constable Crosby had an objection.

He was looking in the direction of the marble plinth.

"It'd still have missed the Fitton Bequest, sir. I'm sure it would. It's too high."

"It could swing easily enough," put in Hepple from his perch outside the window. "You can see that from here. With the bell ropes tethered out of the way like they are, it would have a clear run."

Sloan nodded briskly. "Hepple, can you tell what happened to the end of the twine?"

Hepple squinted at the piece in his hand. "Cut, sir, I should say."

"Not burnt?"

The twine would have to go under a comparison microscope at the Forensic Laboratory but there was still such a thing as the naked eye. Microscopic examination was what it was called but he wouldn't put that in his report. The Superintendent was sensitive to long words.

And there was still the spent match unaccounted for.

Superintendent Leeyes had no time for loose ends either.

"No, sir," Hepple was saying. "It's quite a clean cut. No charring. Could have been scissors or a knife. Something like that."

There was another thing a microscope might be able to do for them. Tell if a heavy weight had strained the fibres of the twine. You never knew with microscopes these days.

"Ah." Nathan Styles's creaking voice started up again.

"B'ain't be the length it is now that counts, is it? It's the length it was afore it was cut . . ."

"That's right, Mr Styles," said Sloan. Crosby shouldn't need a country rustic to spell things out for him like this. "It could have been long enough before it was cut to knock the sculpture off its plinth."

"But why take it away anyway?" asked Crosby mulishly. "Why not leave it there?"

"Because it'd be a dead giveaway," said the old bell-ringer promptly. "Can't you see that, lad? Stands to reason."

"There was a good chance," said Sloan, "that we might miss the twine or not know what it was for."

"It still doesn't tell us how it was done," Crosby persisted obstinately.

"No."

"The chap could have aimed for the sculpture from up here," observed Hepple from the window. "I've got quite a good view."

"You wouldn't have in the dark," said Sloan.

"There was that match . . ." put in Crosby.

Sloan took a deep breath. "There's only one thing we do know . . ."

"Sir?"

"The time the twine was cut and whatever was on the end of it taken away."

"No, we don't, sir . . ." Then his face changed. "Oh, yes, we do . . ." he breathed. "We do. At two o'clock this morning . . ."

"Exactly."

"By the night fisherman those two Metford women said they saw."

"The Metfords? Daft as coots the pair of 'em," remarked Nathan Styles conversationally, "especially Ivy."

Hepple, still at the window, tilted his helmet back. "And who would the night fisherman be, sir, if I might ask?"

"That's why he needed a rod," interrupted Crosby excitedly, waving the churchwarden's stave about in a way not envisaged by the Vicar. "He wouldn't be able to reach it from the window otherwise and we know he couldn't get in through the doors, don't we?"

"What rod?" asked a bewildered Hepple.

"A fisherman's rod, Hepple," explained Sloan kindly. "To çatch the end of the twine. Now we know why he needed a long rod. To hook the twine and take away whatever was hanging at the end of it."

"Ah," said Nathan Styles entering into the spirit of things, "that would have been back in the middle of the tower, by then, wouldn't it?"

"It would," agreed Sloan.

"Dead underneath the bell beam," said the little man. "Gravity would do that."

Sloan nodded. It had been the Superintendent who had said you couldn't interfere with gravity, hadn't it?

Aeons ago.

Or this morning.

They seemed all the same to Sloan now.

"A fisherman's rod would do the trick nicely," said Hepple ponderously, measuring the distance to the middle of the tower with his eye.

"I suppose," said Crosby, sounding doubtful, "that it would have stopped swinging by then . . ."

"I think," said Sloan softly, "that we can take it that it would."

Crosby scratched his head. "You mean that's why he waited until then?"

"I do."

"He knew?"

"I think," said Sloan heavily, "that he worked it out. Just like he worked everything else out." He looked up at the window. "All right, Hepple, you can come down now."

Hepple let go of the twine and withdrew his arm from the embrasure. His face disappeared as he backed down the ladder. The twine—even without anything on the end of it—fell back towards the middle of the tower and then—pendulumlike—swung on through an arc towards the opposite door—the one leading back into the nave and church proper.

Sloan stopped in his tracks.

"Crosby, did you see that?"

"No, sir. What, sir?"

"The twine, man."

"What about it, sir?"

"Crosby, we're fools."

"Yes, sir."

"You didn't notice anything about the way that the twine fell back from the window?"

"No, sir."

"It went towards the door, Crosby. The door. Not the plinth. Don't you see? The window and the sculpture—they aren't in line, are they?"

"No, sir."

"So how did anything on the twine aimed from the window in the dark hit the Fitton Bequest?"

"Search me, sir," said Crosby agreeably.

There was a sudden high cackle from old Nathan Styles.

"Proper mystery, isn't it?"

"You don't have to explain pendulums to me, Sloan," said Superintendent Leeyes testily. "I know all about Galileo."

"Galileo, sir?"

"The chap who chucked two things from the top of the Leaning Tower of Pisa to see which got to the bottom first. I've been there." The Superintendent and his wife had once been to Italy on a package tour and they were never allowed to forget it at the Police Station. "He found out about pendulums."

"What about them, sir?"

Leeyes waved a lofty hand. "The swing of the pendulum always takes exactly the same time whether it's a long swing or a short one."

"Clocks," said Sloan suddenly.

"That sort of thing," agreed Leeyes. "They sent him to prison for it."

"For finding out?"

"Oh, yes," said the Superintendent grandly. "They thought he was a dangerous chap. Had a lot of new ideas."

"I see, sir. A bad lot."

Sloan had so far never been instrumental in sending anyone to prison except for having old ideas—some of them very old indeed.

Cain and Abel old.

Some older than that, too, now he came to think of it . . .

He had got Crosby to drive him back to the police station at Berebury from Randall's Bridge after all. And it was just as well. There had been all manner of messages waiting for him there.

The Airport people in London had traced a passenger called G. Mardoni who had caught a plane to Schiepol in Holland an hour or so after the Rome flight on which he had been booked had left.

The next message had been more useful still and Sloan had taken it in with him to Superintendent Leeyes.

It was from the Guardia de Publica Sicurezza in Rome. They had traced Giuseppe Mardoni from a Dutch flight to his apartment near the Castelsanangelo and were holding him. Please, what would their esteemed friends the Politzei Inglesi like doing with him?

"You'd better acknowledge this quickly, Sloan," instructed Leeyes, whose knowledge of Italian history was hazy (but whose celebrated holiday tour had included Rome), "before they throw him in the Tiber."

"Yes, sir."

"Anything else come in?"

"Details of the two patents. The one which Sergeant Wharton's man found in Blake's room is an old one—registered in the name of Jonah Bernard Struthers before the war. The other is George Osborne's and that's dated yesterday like they said." Far too much happened yesterday for Sloan's liking.

"Appleton's still watching Osborne, I hope."

"He is."

"Anything else?"

"The link with Hallworthy's Small Motors. Someone's been quick . . ."

"Ah . . ." The Superintendent stretched his arms in a way that was positively feline.

"Paul Blake."

Leeyes rubbed his hands together. "Blake, eh?"

"Hallworthy's Small Motors were his last employers but one."

"Were they, indeed?" said Leeyes silkily, the cat-and-mouse touch even more apparent now.

"The last people he worked for were bought out by Hallworthy's a year ago."

Leeyes pounced. "Then he came to Struthers and Tindall and Hallworthy's tried to buy Struthers and Tindall?"

"Could be. But Tindall wouldn't sell. At least, not to the highest bidder."

"So someone kills Tindall . . ."

"Tindall was killed, sir, but we don't know exactly how or why yet."

"What's all this business about pendulums for then?"

Sloan shook his head. "I don't think a pendulum would necessarily do the trick, sir. The sculpture was off-line from the window."

"Well," said the Superintendent, leaning comfortably back in his chair, "seeing that there's no such thing as an eccentric pendulum you'd better go away and have another think, hadn't you?"

As he walked back down the corridor to his own room a little *frisson* of cold trickled down Sloan's spine . . .

Then his head came up . . .

There was such a thing as an eccentric pendulum.

He'd seen it.

In a museum somewhere.

He and Margaret. It had something to do with the earth's gravity pulling it to one side or something like that.

But only if the cord was long enough.

Long enough?

Seventy or eighty feet. It had to be something like that.

Seventy feet! whispered a little voice in Sloan's brain.

Inspector Harpe loped by him in the corridor but Sloan didn't see him.

It was coming back to him now.

If he remembered rightly the only thing this particular

pendulum needed was a long drop and a smooth start and half an hour later it was right off course. Pulled by the earth's gravity.

The smooth start had been important. He remembered that, too. It had to be released very carefully indeed. No jerk or push or anything like that. In fact he remembered standing with Margaret while a man from the Museum came along and started it by burning away the anchoring string with a match.

By burning it with a match . . .

A match.

A perfectly ordinary match.

"Crosby!" He pushed open the door of his room.

"Sir?"

"Get me the Metropolitan Police. And quickly."

"Yes, sir." As the Detective Constable picked up the telephone he pushed two more message sheets in Sloan's direction. "There's something in from Constable Appleton, sir. George Osborne's left the Grammar School in Berebury and he thinks he's heading out for Cleete . . ."

"Is that Mets?" asked Sloan in the telephone.

"The other," persisted Crosby, undeflected, "is from Luston Police. They haven't turned up anything useful so far at United Mellemetics."

"Mets?" said Sloan urgently. "Now, look here—I want you to send someone round to a museum for me. Yes, that's right. A museum. And then I want you to put me on to someone who can explain a patent to me . . . an old patent . . ."

... I HAVE COMMITTED
SOME SECRET DEED WHICH I DESIRE THE
WORLD MAY NEVER HEAR OF.

◆

21

Dr Dabbe was on the telephone and still concerned with the late Sir Digby Wellow.

"I can't add a lot to what I told you in the car park, Sloan, except that his coronary arteries weren't a lot to write home about. Good for a few more business lunches and public speeches but not all that many if that's any consolation to Lady Wellow. As to the wound ..."

"Yes?"

"It is the same in every recognisable respect," said the pathologist in the measured terms he used in court, "as that inflicted on Richard Tindall. The only variation is in the amount of force used. Everything points to it being the same weapon. What's that, Sloan ... do I happen to know anything about what?"

"Foucault's Pendulum," said Sloan confidently.

The Metropolitan Police had already rung him back from London. They'd been round to the Museum for him.

"Let me see now ..." The pathologist paused. "Foucault's Pendulum ... Isn't that the one used for demonstrating the rotation of the earth on its own axis?"

"That's the one," said Sloan.

Explaining it to Superintendent Leeyes wasn't going to be as easy as this.

Or to Crosby.

Perhaps he wouldn't even try.

Perhaps he'd just put it into his report for the Superintendent and bank on Crosby not wanting to know.

"I remember." Dr Dabbe's interest quickened. "Actually the swing of the pendulum stays the same . . ."

"Galileo," put in Sloan. The Superintendent would like that.

". . . and it's the earth which moves but, of course, it doesn't look like that."

"No."

His voice changed. "I say, Sloan, are you onto something?"

"Perhaps," responded Sloan temperately. "It would explain the spent match we found. I couldn't fit it in with anything else."

"How?"

"When demonstrating Foucault's Pendulum you have to set it off very carefully indeed. That's the whole secret. Without a jerk. You do it by mooring whatever's on the end—say a metal ball—something heavy anyway—to something fixed."

"Say the bars of a small window?" said Dabbe drily.

"That would do very nicely," agreed Sloan.

There was a man from the Area Forensic Laboratory already on his way to the church at Randall's Bridge with the sort of magnifying glass that Sherlock Holmes might have dreamt of. He was going to look at the metal bars of the embrasure window. You never knew what might have left its mark there.

Dyson, the police photographer, was on his way to the church, too.

He had been detailed by Sloan to take pictures of a length of black twine dangling from the bell beam.

"Black twine, Inspector?" he had echoed. "You must be joking. It doesn't even smile when you say 'cheese' let alone watch the birdie."

"I have reason to believe," Sloan had told him austerely, "that it was an instrument of death."

"There!" cried the incorrigible Dyson in tones of

mock disappointment, "and I'd been putting my money on an orangoutang . . ."

"What you usually do to set off Foucault's Pendulum," Sloan said now to the pathologist, "is to burn through the string which anchors it at the start of its swing."

"So you do," agreed Dabbe. "I'd forgotten that bit."

"Whoever started it off—if that is what did the trick— must have dropped the match while he was reaching through the little window."

"Foucault's Pendulum takes time, you know, Sloan. It doesn't go out of line straightaway. I can't remember the details—not my field, really. Is it something like one degree in five minutes?"

"Twelve degrees in an hour, Doctor, in London." Sloan faithfully repeated what the man from the Museum had said to the man from Mets. "It was the question of time which put me on to it."

"Time? What has time to do with it?"

"I think our villain wanted time. That's the only explanation which makes sense. Otherwise why kill Tindall where he did—let alone how. And why not kill him outright when he hit him the first time?"

"Good point, Sloan. Sir Digby's dead enough."

"The usual reason," said Sloan, "for wanting time is to establish an alibi."

But the pathologist was still thinking about the pendulum. "It would be a nice calculation, Sloan. You'd take your twelve degrees an hour plus the length of your pendulum and its first swing and I daresay you'd need to know the weight of whatever you put on the end. What do you think that was, by the way?"

"Something heavy," said Sloan. "It would need to weigh thirty pounds at least."

The Museum had told Mets that, too.

"Then," said Dabbe more energetically still, "you'd have to work out how far over you must tilt your statue so that the first knock from the weight of the pendulum would knock it over . . ."

Sloan cleared his throat. "I thought, Doctor, you said that given enough factors you could do any equation . . ."

"A hit," cried the pathologist delightedly, "a palpable hit. Tell me more . . ."

Sloan put the telephone back and picked up something from his desk.

"Come on, Crosby. We don't want to waste any time now."

"To Cleete, sir?"

"Certainly not," said Sloan militantly, striding down the corridor. "Not now that we know that those emerald and diamond clips were for Mrs Osborne . . ."

The constable was faint but pursuing. "Where to, sir?"

"Struthers and Tindall, of course. Where did you think?"

What Sloan had picked up from his desk had been a warrant for murder.

After he had executed it he stood in front of Richard Tindall's desk in Richard Tindall's office. On his left were Miss Hilda Holroyd, Paul Blake, and Gordon Cranswick. On his right, hastily summoned from Cleete, were Fenella Tindall, and George and Marcia Osborne.

Sloan pointed to Richard Tindall's desk and said, "Big desk, big man." Then he waved his arm in the direction of the corridor leading towards Henry Pysden's room. "Big desk, little man."

He was speaking metaphorically.

They all knew that.

Henry Pysden had fought like a tiger when they arrested him. It had needed all of Sergeant Wharton's massive strength as well as Crosby's weight to take him away.

"It all began," said Sloan, "when an old patent belonging to Struthers and Tindall became important in a new manufacturing process."

"Better to buy the firm," said the owner of Cranswick Processing unabashed, "than fork out a royalty every time we used Struthers and Tindall's patent."

"Hallworthy's Small Motors thought so, too, sir," said Sloan evenly, "and they went a bit further than you did. They insinuated Mr Blake here into the firm to find out what he could to help the sale along."

Paul Blake turned an uncomfortable red.

Fenella Tindall, who had no colour at all in her face, turned to him. "You were nothing but a spy then?"

"However," intervened Sloan hastily, "neither Hallworthy's nor Cranswick Processing were prepared to give unconditional guarantees about keeping staff on and that was Richard Tindall's death warrant. He found out about Paul Blake being an agent of Hallworthy's, didn't like their methods, and so opted in favour of Cranswick . . ."

"But why?" asked Marcia Osborne. "Why did he want to sell at all . . ."

Sloan cleared his throat. "His wife had died and I think he guessed that he might be losing his daughter, too, soon."

"Me?" said Fenella, two pink spots appearing on her cheeks.

"Fair stood the wind for Italy," said George Osborne, speaking for the first time. He had a lean, intelligent face and had listened attentively so far. "That right, Inspector?"

And it was Fenella's turn to blush.

"If you inherited the firm, miss, there was a good chance that Henry Pysden might be left to carry on or at least negotiate the new sale."

George Osborne stirred. "Inspector, I don't quite see where United Mellemetics comes into all this."

"It doesn't, sir. Not at all. I think we would find that there was nothing wrong with the United Mellemetics file . . ."

"But what about poor Sir Digby Wellow . . ." that was Marcia Osborne.

"I'm afraid, Mrs Osborne, that he died in the cause of . . ." Sloan searched for the right word.

George Osborne supplied it. "Verisimilitude."

"Very probably, sir."

"The file, though," said Miss Holroyd, the perfect secretary. "I don't quite understand about the file, Inspector."

"It did disappear but that I'm afraid was only because Henry Pysden took it. I expect it's in the river by now. You put me on to that, miss."

"Me?" said Miss Holroyd.

"You said you weren't present when Pysden told me he handed it over to Mr Tindall yesterday. When I went back over everything to do with that file I found that all our so-called mysterious information about it stemmed only from Henry Pysden."

Miss Holroyd frowned. "But he said Mr Tindall said . . ."

"Only they weren't quotes at all," pointed out Sloan. "The works foreman and Mr Blake here"—he looked with disfavour at the young scientist—"both found their work on it completely routine so I checked back in case it was a red herring."

"And it was?" Fenella was beginning to look more animated by the minute. "You mean he killed poor Sir Digby Wellow just to . . . to . . . to lend a touch of colour to the killing of my father?"

"To divert suspicion to United Mellemetics anyway, miss."

"How could he!" she exclaimed.

"And the copy of the patent in Mr Blake's room, Inspector?" Miss Holroyd's tidy mind seized on a second loose end.

"Another red herring. Though at that stage, of course," remarked Sloan pleasantly, "it still left Mr Blake here in the running for double murder."

Paul Blake started to stutter. "H—h—hhh—how come?"

It was Gordon Cranswick, the businessman, who answered him. "Tindall could have rumbled you, boy, and you might have killed him to keep him quiet."

Paul Blake's handsomeness wasn't quite so apparent now. "I wouldn't . . ."

"We know you wouldn't," said Gordon Cranswick briskly, "but the Inspector couldn't be sure of that then."

"Not at that particular point," agreed Sloan suavely.

"When then?" demanded the young scientist hotly.

Sloan cleared his throat. "When I started thinking about alibis for the killing of Richard Tindall."

"I hadn't got one," retorted Blake upon the instant.

"I know." Sloan nodded. "Nobody had an alibi except

Henry Pysden and oddly enough his was cast iron. A signature tied up to a machine which was double sealed."

"Copper-bottomed," observed Gordon Cranswick, in the language of Lloyds.

"Too much of a good thing?" suggested George Osborne more perceptively.

"Much too much," agreed Sloan. "Unfortunately the Cranswick takeover played into his hands."

"Why?" demanded the Chairman and Managing Director of Cranswick Processing Limited.

"I gather that cloak and dagger meetings, exaggerated secrecy, cryptic messages and so forth are all part and parcel of these deals . . ."

"Practically standard practice," the businessman assured him readily.

"I should imagine this lent a certain amount of credence to any message Henry Pysden used to lure Richard Tindall to the church tower late last night."

"The telephone call," breathed Marcia Osborne.

"Not about Cranswick Processing, Inspector," said Gordon Cranswick.

"No, sir." Sloan coughed. "Would I be very wrong though if I suggested that if Pysden had said that Sir Digby Wellow wanted to see him in that particular place and time that Richard Tindall would have believed him?"

"That clown . . ." began Cranswick and then remembered that he, too, was dead, and fell silent.

"The message only had to be believable when Henry Pysden gave it to him. That's all. Nothing else. He could have dreamed up anything he liked. From then on it was all plain sailing."

"I should like to know how," said Fenella Tindall steadily, "and then I should like to go home."

"You're coming back with us," said George Osborne in a matter-of-fact way which brooked no contradiction.

Marcia Osborne seconded this with a nod. Her diamond and emerald jewellery didn't fit in at Struthers and Tindall either.

Sloan didn't mind. Not now.

He took a deep breath and began, "There was one important factor which was common knowledge . . ."

* * *

". . . that, sir, was the work being done in the church at Randall's Bridge." Sloan had to repeat it all to the Superintendent back at the Police Station. "They had to advertise the moving of the Fitton Bequest—the Church Secretary told us that—when they got a faculty for all the changes in the church."

Leeyes grunted.

"And it wasn't unreasonable for Pysden to suppose," continued Sloan smoothly, "that a pathologist would be able to work out the time of Tindall's death fairly accurately. They're getting better at it all the time."

Leeyes grunted again.

"So any time after Evensong on Sunday Pysden rigs up his pendulum, does the calculations so that it knocks the statue over at eleven-thirty, then last night—the day before Tindall is due to sign on the dotted line Pysden gets a message that Gordon Cranswick or Sir Digby Wellow or Genghis Khan wants to see him in the tower at Randall's Bridge—or some such tale . . . that's another point against him, by the way, sir . . ."

"What is?" growled Leeyes unhelpfully.

"That sort of message must have come from someone like Pysden whom Tindall really trusted or he wouldn't have acted on it. Catch me going to a church tower at midnight."

"If I asked you to," said Leeyes pointedly, "I take it you would."

"Naturally," said Sloan hastily. "Of course, sir. So Pysden waits for him in the church tower, knocks him out and sets the pendulum going."

"Nasty."

"Pysden drives Tindall's car back to its garage at Cleete —which is about the only place where it wouldn't cause comment—collects his own car which he probably left somewhere in Cleete—Hepple's checking on that now— and then hurries back to the works in Berebury to establish his alibi. He's got half an hour and it all works out very nicely."

"H'mmm."

"All he had to do is come back for the lead weight."

Sloan coughed. "And killing Sir Digby was—er—just gilding the lily."

"Another assignation?"

"Child's play, I expect. Pysden would only have to hint at something fishy in the United Mellemetics file and Sir Digby would meet him anywhere."

"What about the Italian?" said Leeyes gamely. "All you've said about gain applies to him too."

"His visit was unexpected," said Sloan. "Mrs Turvey, the daily woman at Cleete, told us so. And this murder was—er—calculated."

"I always said," trumpeted the Superintendent, "that you couldn't play about with gravity."

"Anyway, sir," said Sloan hastily, "at two o'clock this morning Giuseppe Mardoni was at the Airport—not retrieving a lead weight from the pendulum in the church tower with a fishing rod."

"The girl could have done that," suggested Leeyes: but half-heartedly.

"She's going to sell out to Cranswick after she's been advised about the value of this old patent . . ."

It was Detective Constable Crosby who disturbed them.

"No news about those shoes on the golf course yet, sir, but there are two more anonymous letters in from Culling-oak." He grinned. "The one about the Vicar's wife is rather good, actually."

The Superintendent's face turned a choleric shade of purple.

Crosby didn't notice. He plunged on.

"And the Town Clerk's on the telephone. They think it was sugar in the Mayor's petrol tank this time . . ."

"What's he going to plead?" enquired Dr Dabbe with mild interest.

"I've heard that the Defence have got a psychiatrist lined up," said Sloan.

"Old hat," remarked the pathologist amiably. "Head-shrinkers and trick cyclists are on their way out."

Sloan cocked a mocking eyebrow at the pathologist. "Seeing something nasty in the woodshed isn't why you hit old ladies over the head after all?"

" 'Fraid not."

"And what," enquired Detective Inspector Sloan, quondam law enforcement officer, cautiously, "is on its way in?"

"A new version of original sin, old chap."

"There isn't one."

"Oh, yes, there is. It's called body chemistry."

"What's that?"

"Chromosomes, for a start. And a lot more."

Sloan paused for thought. "Is that better or worse?"

The pathologist chuckled. "Worse, Sloan. Much worse. Nobody can argue with a biochemist . . ."

Detective Constable Crosby dumped the last file of statements down on Sloan's desk. "That's the lot, sir. Including the receipt from Adamson's."

"Crosby . . ."

"Sir?"

"Crosby, did you by any remote chance notice anything out of the ordinary about the Osborne's house when you went there?"

"No, sir," promptly.

"Think."

"Yes, sir."

"Anything?"

"No, sir."

"The mantelpiece," suggested Sloan with a heavy patience. "Did you notice anything about the mantelpiece?"

Crosby screwed up his eyes. "No, sir."

"No birthday cards?" It was almost a plea.

"Oh, yes, sir. A whole row . . ." His voice faltered. "Very pretty, they were."

"If, Crosby," said Sloan letting out a long sigh, "you can't be a good example, then you'll just have to be a horrible warning, that's all."

ABOUT THE AUTHOR

CATHERINE AIRD had never tried her hand at writing suspense stories before publishing *The Religious Body*— a novel which immediately established her as one of the genre's most talented writers. *A Late Phoenix, The Stately Home Murder, His Burial Too, Some Die Eloquent, Henrietta Who?* and *A Most Contagious Game* have subsequently enhanced her reputation. Her ancestry is Scottish, but she now lives in a village in East Kent, near Canterbury, where she serves as an aid to her father, a doctor, and takes an interest in local affairs.